Eagle Rising

Eagle Rising

David Devereux

GOLLANCZ
LONDON

Copyright © David Devereux 2009
All rights reserved

The right of David Devereux to be identified as the author
of this work has been asserted by him in accordance with the
Copyright, Designs and Patents Act 1988.

First published in Great Britain in 2009 by Gollancz
An imprint of the Orion Publishing Group
Orion House, 5 Upper St Martin's Lane,
London WC2H 9EA
An Hachette UK Company

A CIP catalogue record for this book
is available from the British Library

ISBN 978 0 575 07987 8 (Cased)
ISBN 978 0 575 07988 5 (Trade Paperback)

1 3 5 7 9 10 8 6 4 2

Typeset by Input Data Services Ltd,
Bridgwater, Somerset

Printed and bound in the UK
by CPI Mackays, Chatham, Kent

The Orion Publishing Group's policy is to use papers
that are natural, renewable and recyclable products and
made from wood grown in sustainable forests. The logging
and manufacturing processes are expected to conform to
the environmental regulations of the country of origin.

www.orionbooks.co.uk

A Note from the Author

Well, here we are again. Talk about the 'Difficult Second Album', this one had some really interesting moments between synopsis and finished draft. Hopefully it's worked out to everyone's satisfaction. First off, though, I'd like to state the (hopefully) obvious:

**ALL THE MAGIC IN THIS BOOK IS FAKE.
DON'T TRY THIS AT HOME!**

Some people need it spelled out this clearly, so there you are. In fact, if you read this story and it makes you want to be like the characters, stop and take a good look at yourself. Fact and fiction are very different things, and this is most definitely the latter, so do us both a favour and get a grip, OK? Dennis Wheatley used to put a warning in the front of his books about what could happen to those who got mixed up in the occult. He was right to do so, too, but I'll do you a deal: if you use your brain I won't lecture you about how awful the occult can be, and that seems like a fair compromise to me.

Now for the thanks. No man is an island, and I certainly couldn't write this stuff without the assistance of an elite group of freaks and weirdos. It is therefore appropriate that I share the blame, and mention . . .

Steve Jackson, who keeps his place at the top of the list – and not just because my entry into all this authory nonsense was his idea. He's been a great help to me as I've fumbled my way through the world of publishing, and is a bloody good mate on top of all that. If you've ever wondered how this rubbish gets published, ask Steve, and then talk to . . .

Simon Spanton at Gollancz and **Robert Caskie** of Macfarlane Chard Associates, my editor and agent respectively, for services above and beyond the call of duty and for somehow continuing to put up with the scary bald weirdo and his strange ideas. Their patience in difficult circumstances has been such as to shame a saint.

In no particular order: Liz Taylor, Cat Vincent, Chris Bell, Roger Burton West, Diana Wynne Jones, Tom Lloyd, Robert Rankin and, of course, the ever-present friends who'd prefer to stay anonymous.

The unexpected guests in Chapter Twenty-Three are for Robert's fan club, Sproutlore, who'll know why if they were at the post-wedding shenanigans.

Finally, an apology. Last time, I forgot to thank **Lisa Rogers**, who copy-edited *Hunter's Moon* and helped fix several points that weren't quite right, then went on to look after this one as well. Thanks, Lisa, and I hope you'll forgive me.

This book is dedicated to the memory of my mother, who died between its completion and production.

Best wishes,
David Devereux
London, 31st October 2007

Introit

It's a beautiful summer's night, warm and balmy. The sky's a touch clearer than I'd like, though: I can still see the rapidly diminishing shape of the aircraft I jumped out of thirty seconds ago if I turn my head, a dark silhouette against the stars shining brightly in a blue velvet sky. Looking straight ahead, I can see Scotland. Quite a lot of Scotland, in fact, since I'm about twenty thousand feet away from it – and closing rapidly.

There are any number of things I hate about my job, and not many that give me pleasure. One of the latter category is skydiving: the noble art of throwing yourself out of a perfectly good aeroplane and plummeting towards the ground at one hundred and twenty miles an hour. For a few blissful minutes it's just you and the sky, which gives a man time to relax and think without interruptions apart from the occasional hope that your parachute doesn't fail, since there's a very good reason why they call it *terminal* velocity.

My thoughts on this particular occasion are on what's going to happen when I land. Discounting the option of becoming a large red stain on the landscape, because if that happens there's not much else to worry about apart from Final Judgement and a quick trip to Hell (or wherever), I have a castle to deal with. All I have to do is get in, get hold of a small, portable object and get out again without anyone noticing. It's a piece of piss, really.

The castle's guarded, of course: men, sensors and probably a few other things as well are all conspiring to interrupt my progress and ruin my night's work, but I'm sanguine. This is a thing that can be done; it's simply a matter of doing it. I have floor plans; I know exactly where I'm going and how I'm getting home again; I've even got the times when the guards change shifts, which is why I'm arriving just before shift change in the middle of the night: the guards will be tired and bored, and their sharp, well-rested relief is still another twenty minutes away.

About a thousand feet off the deck I pull the ripcord and breathe a sigh of relief as a sheet of dark bluish-grey fabric almost exactly the same shade as the sky opens above me with a crack. Watch the ground coming up to meet me in the last few seconds, then bend my knees and roll when I hit the ground. Gather up the parachute and hide it under a bush quickly, before anyone who might have decided to investigate my arrival happens by to find the proof, then into the heather and round the hill to my destination.

It's a short walk from here, and I'm grateful for the cover among all these bushes. There was a time when this land would have been cleared to make it easy for the castle's defenders to spot oncoming trouble, but since nobody attacks castles in the twenty-first century, that kind of clearance would have been noticed by the outside world. These days the lookouts are armed with infrared scopes and motion detectors, and these are still things that can be easily defeated with a bit of know-how.

I'm collecting foliage on the way and adding it to my gear to serve as a little extra camouflage. Pre-done camo is pretty good these days (certainly it's come on in leaps and bounds during the last few years) but there's still no substitute for using the local landscape to hide you and there are a number of ways to do that. My favourite has always been sticking bits of it onto me so I look a bit like a walking bush. If I was a couple of feet taller I suppose I could be a walking tree – very *Macbeth*, given where I am. Hail,

Jack, miserable bastard, who shall be cold and irritable hereafter.

Naah: doesn't scan.

Onwards, as ever. To the castle.

It's not exactly a swift trip. I've given myself ninety minutes to get from the edge of visual range to the base of the walls, and while I've got no reason to suspect ground microphones (which would leave me well and truly stuffed the moment I stepped into range) the briefing had made it very clear that they still use old-fashioned lookouts as well as technology to guard their perimeter. So patience is the key: move slowly and carefully so the guards' eyes aren't drawn to my neck of the gorse. I'm not as quiet as I'd like, either, but that's another factor I can't do much about. Moving slowly can only reduce the sounds of my passage, not eliminate them entirely.

Eighty-six minutes later, I arrive at the base of the castle walls. I'm scratched to buggery through my gear thanks to the delightful local flora but don't detect any signs of actual bleeding. This is a good thing, since that kind of evidence would just be embarrassing when it came to working out who'd robbed the place and where he was afterwards. Time to lose the bushy look and turn back into ninja-boy: matt-black clothing, webbing tight against my body and weapons in handy places should I need them. Now all I have to do is get up a thirty-foot-high wall.

This is usually the bit in the film when the hero throws a grappling hook, which catches perfectly (and quietly) in just the right spot on the first throw. Trouble is, that doesn't work in the real world. For a start, you almost never get it right first time. Then there's the fact that these things are made of metal, and the wall's made of stone. You guessed it: that makes noise. Even if we assume all that works the way the movies tell you, it still starts with me throwing a moderately heavy lump of metal thirty feet straight up. I'm not unhandy, but do me a favour, will you?

I'm not even going to start about the joys of the rope coming off this hypothetical grapnel because, frankly, if you still think I'm going with that plan you've obviously not been paying attention. The whole bloody idea is a dumb one and we're not going to discuss it any further. There are plenty of handholds to be had, so I'm climbing up as nature intended – even if the architects might prefer I didn't.

Slow, sure and silent, moving hand then foot, making my way up the wall. A slip would be embarrassing – nobody wants to be captured at the bottom of a wall with their legs broken. People would laugh. Four storeys to climb and all the time in the world to do it. The first storey's barely work, and the second's easy enough. By the third my fingers are starting to let me know that they're not overly keen on holding two hundred pounds of bastard, and by the fourth they're considering forming a union and going on strike. Lucky for me they're about as organised as any other union and are still trying to elect a shop steward by the time I get to the top. There's broken glass up here, but I've got a Kevlar blanket rolled up on my back that makes nifty work of this kind of situation. Two toeholds, one hand somewhere safe and the other throws the blanket into position for me to scramble over. Roll it up again, put it back in its place and survey the roof.

The moon's on my side here – I can just about make out tripwires criss-crossing the tiles. I don't think there are pressure sensors up here and I can't hear any signs of alarm yet so it's just a matter of care and methodical movement to get across to the chimney. Run a bypass on the alarm sensors, using a couple of wires and some crocodile clips to connect a black box from the geeks back home, then it's out with the wire cutters to remove the mesh covering the top. It's good stuff, but then so are my cutters – I sharpened them myself just a few hours ago.

Now for the rope. I can belay myself on the chimney stack, by the look of it, and I know how far it needs to drop inside to give me an easy lower down. I stick a bar across the centre to make sure I can get down without picking up any soot and then start lowering myself like a kid in one of the Charles Dickens books I never read at school.

I end up in an unused bedroom, the fireplace cold in the darkness. A few seconds to make sure I missed the soot and it's over to the door. Thick wood, but I can't hear movement outside when I stick my ear to the crack at the bottom. It's fully lit out there, so I flash my torch into my eyes a couple of times to pre-adjust my sight for it. No point getting caught while I can't see.

The corridor's about what you'd expect: long, wide, stone and decorated with the occasional tapestry. My host likes to live well and has pretensions to being a laird, even though I understand that the locals think he's a nasty little nouveau-riche Saxon fuckbag who should bugger off back to England. He can, for all I care, once I've finished here. For some reason the Boss has decided that I'm to leave him be – leave everyone be if I can – so he can spend the next six months looking under the furniture to see where his valued possession has got to.

Down the corridor, following my planned route. This is the second floor, where the nobs sleep, and I need to be one floor down and halfway across the house. Piece of piss.

The stairway's empty, but I know that there are dogs let loose downstairs so it's not a surprise. Slowly working my way down, at the outer edges of the steps to maximise my view down the spiral. Make it all the way, step out and listen. Good, I can't hear the dogs. Out with a small metal box, and open it to reveal two pre-filled metal syringes inside. I only need one for the moment – up against the dining-room door and squirt the liquid underneath it. Urine from a bitch in heat should keep the furry bastards distracted while I go about my business. I can hear paws coming towards me now, so I head off in the other direction while putting the case away.

A nice stealthy walk, the long way of course, gets me to the library door and its fingerprint lock. I know the make, the model and its weakness, and came prepared. One false fingertip goes on with a little gum, is pressed up to the sensor and a second later there's a green light and a gentle click that lets me know I'm in.

I pull out the Kevlar blanket again, then it's through the door and up against the wall as slowly as I possibly can. There's a movement sensor in here and I need a second to prepare the way past it. I unroll the blanket, taking my time to get it right while my eyes adjust to the reduced light level, then move it into position between me and the sensor. Now I can breathe again – the sensor picks up on moving heat sources and the blanket masks mine very nicely indeed. Still moving cautiously, I make my way up to the sensor and cover it with the blanket. Lovely.

So here we are in the library. Somewhere around here is a safe, in which I should find what I'm looking for. Fortunately, I know that the safe is hidden behind a row of books – which is an enormous help when you're standing in a room with about twenty thousand of the fuckers. Strangely enough, nobody bothered to tell me *which* bloody books I'm supposed to be looking for.

Oh, how I love my job sometimes.

I have to hope that the metal detector I brought with me is sensitive enough to find the safe without telling me about every pipe and wire as well. Time's a-wasting, and while I might act as if there's all the time in the world, there's still a rendezvous I need to make unless I fancy walking all the way back to Inverness.

Which I don't.

No point fannying around with worries about my lift now, so I get the metal detector out and start scanning the shelves I can reach. Five minutes later there's no joy, so I have to work the upper levels. Up the ladders, then, and give thanks for them being well-enough maintained that they don't squeak. This bit takes longer, since I'm moving each ladder along the wall as I go, and after fifteen minutes of up, sweep, down and move the ladder on all four walls I have the sure and certain knowledge that this gadget is a piece of shit.

Time to look for secret switches. Nothing in the desk, or the display cabinet full of weird Japanese tentacle sculptures. Check the sculptures, and discover that a bust of some old git has a lift-up head with a switch underneath it. Stupid bastard had to be a Batman fan, didn't he? The panel I seek opens up and there's the safe.

At least he's enough of a traditionalist to use a key-operated safe, which puts him back up a notch in my book. I'm carrying kit for all eventualities here, but lock-picks are a particular thing of mine and I like a nice challenge. This is a job for sensitivity, training and talent – all things I have in spades.

All I need to open a safe like this old beastie are time, patience and a few pieces of wire. And luck – in the hope that they haven't retrofitted it with a trip guard or some other kind of anti-pick mechanism. It's difficult to tell from the outside, but the sensations coming down the picks to my fingertips are all as they should be. It's a subtle process, with a lot of levers to catch and hold in just the right position, but I'm comfortable with what I'm doing and a few minutes' work yields results as I feel the assembly slip into place, and I slowly rotate my wrist to shift the bolts back. Now turn the handle, open the door and . . .

There it is.

A slim, hand-written volume of notes by a notorious black magician. The original's believed to be in the Vatican, who aren't saying either way, but this is thought to be the only copy, taken down painstakingly by his apprentice only a couple of months before an angry mob stormed their house with the time-honoured pitchforks and burning torches. It's priceless, irreplaceable, and coming with me.

Close the safe carefully, go through all the rigmarole of locking it again and then close the panel and put the old git's head back on. Bedtime for bastards, I think – the clock's ticking and I've got a lift to catch.

Having checked that everything's back as I found it, I grab the blanket and reverse course towards the door. Slow and steady again, slide the door open and move into the corridor. Roll up the blanket, and start back. I'm toying with a couple of ways out at the moment, but the best still looks like more or less the way I came, which will let me get rid of the rope. Not much I can do about replacing the grille over the chimney (my weight allowance didn't have room for portable welding gear) but there's no sense in leaving any more clues than I have to. I head upstairs with the help of a second staircase – don't want to disturb the pooches – and move into the corridor.

Hello, Mr Guard, I wasn't expecting to see you here. Ever heard of the Vulcan death grip? Apparently not – let's find somewhere quiet for you to have a nice lie down.

I hoist the now slightly less attentive guard over my shoulder and tramp back towards the room I started out from. There's no point making it too easy to find him even if I have just blown my beautifully covert little run. Hopefully they'll think he's stopped for a piss or something rather than raising the alarm just yet. All I need is another five minutes to get up that chimney and then I'm gone.

Back into the bedroom. I lay the guard out on the bed as though he's taking a sneaky nap and move back to the chimney. Hunting for the rope . . .

And finding a door covering my way out. Steel. Solid. Locked. Oh crap.

Over to the window, pull the latch back, swear as it fails to open. Must be some kind of lock built into the frame.

Double crap.

Escape plan number two: back downstairs. Out the door and towards the stairs, moving as quickly as I can. Coming round the corner I surprise another guard, and I've punched him hard enough to put him on his backside before the thought's cleared its way across my head. A quick finishing move that should leave his neck nicely snapped and his spinal cord severed concludes matters quickly enough. He just about fits in a cleaning cupboard and I'm moving again. Things have now officially turned into the shape of a pear and my only priority is getting the hell out of here intact.

I dismiss the bedroom window on the grounds that it's glazed with laminated security stuff that would make a racket to get through. The doors on the ground floor are going to be locked, so the most likely escape route is another chimney. Racking my memory for another unoccupied room, I find one within reach. In, over to the chimney and take a look.

Also blocked with a steel door.

The bastards are on to me. They must be.

Fine. Gloves off, then – I can safely dispense with the sneaking around and get creative.

Despite my orders to keep it quiet, I did manage to find room for a line of detcord in my gear. Over to the window, try the usual way of opening without success, and start laying the explosive round the edge. Piece of cake. Next, to the bed, and start turning the sheets into an emergency rope of strips knotted together. Judging by how much trouble they give me I think I should be OK to get down them intact. Tie one end to the enormous bed, loop the rest around my arm ready to throw out of the window and move back to light the fuse on the detcord.

The door bangs open suddenly, and I feel the first round hit my left leg as I'm turning to face it. Another hits me in the chest, then one in my shoulder.

'Gotcha!' The guard looks far too pleased with himself, pleased enough that I want to wipe the smile off his face with sandpaper. 'That'll be an "Exercise Over", then.'

'Bollocks. How did you get me?' I ask, wiping a splash of paint off my chin.

'The dogs didn't show up for their late-night feeding. That set us looking.'

'Bloody typical. Oh well, any chance of a cup of tea?'

Chapter One

You don't want to know who I am.

No, really: you don't. The last person who went digging for my real name was found dead in a ditch so thoroughly messed up that his own mother didn't recognise what was left of the body. The people who know me and like me – and know what I do for a living – call me Jack. Most of them are dead, though, which makes trips to the pub a bit of a challenge.

It was another summer's day in London: hot, sweaty and possessed of an atmosphere you could cut with a blunt knife. The call had summoned me to an old office building on the edge of the City, the kind where dodgy back-room deals are handled by millionaires in slightly tatty suits and shoes in desperate need of new heels. The kind of place where nobody looks you in the eye, just in case they have to testify about seeing you when the Fraud Squad come looking. Down a corridor in serious need of a new strip light, checking over my shoulder for any observers, and in through a door marked 'Maintenance'.

The office beyond was identical to every other office I'd ever met the Boss in, as though all of them were the same room reached through different doors. The same desk, the same telephones, the same evil old man sitting there staring at me like I'd just been scraped off the front bumper of his vintage Rolls-Royce. Time to sit down and take my briefing like a man.

'I want you to take a look at something,' he said, skipping the formalities and getting straight to work as always. 'Special Branch raided a bedsit in Camden last night and found some papers they didn't understand. They passed them on to MI5, who were equally lacking in comprehension, so now they're on their way to GCHQ for decryption.' He pushed a folder across the desk: light blue, for analysis, and about half an inch thick. It made a pleasant change to see one of those instead of the red folders with orders to kill that feature all too bloody frequently in my life.

'Won't they be missed, sir?'

'No, because you're the courier. There's a car waiting for you downstairs, so you'd better work fast or hope for bad traffic. I want your report in the morning. Dismissed.'

'Sir.' End of interview and out the door, holding a brown envelope with MI5 markings and a cargo of who-knows-what. Time to hope for bad traffic, indeed.

The car turned out to be a minicab, or at least a pretty good impersonation of one. I sat in the back as we fought our way through London traffic, documents open on my lap and spread across the seat.

It started out with some fairly tasty neo-Nazi propaganda, the usual bullshit about how all the wogs should go back where they came from and leave Britain to the British. That made me laugh – we're such a bunch of mongrels these days that I don't honestly think anyone can claim to be 100% anything any more. Besides, how far do you want to take it back? To the Windrush generation? World War Two? The French Revolution? William the Conqueror? Angles and Saxons? *Romani ite domum*, that's what I say. We were doing just fine until they showed up with their suntans, decent roads and functional irrigation systems, the bastards.

Leafing through the bullshit, stifling the occasional giggle where it was particularly badly written, managed to kill about three-quarters of an hour and a third of the pile. Nothing unusual, though – certainly nothing that would make it worth sending to GCHQ, and certainly nothing that would deserve my attention.

We pulled into an anonymous car park somewhere in London, and I gathered the papers back into the file. Here was my 'official' ride: a nice, comfy saloon car that didn't smell slightly of stale chips, which was a distinct improvement on the vehicle I'd been travelling in thus far. I was already suited up from having to be in the City, so it was just a matter of getting comfy on the nice leather-backed seat before my driver fired up the engine and started sliding towards the south-west like a hot knife through butter. Fast, quiet and efficient: three words I'm very fond of, and it's always nice to see a professional doing what they're really good at. This guy, for example, could have made a lot of money in the bank-blagging business if his current performance was anything to go by. He reminded me of my own driving instructor, a quiet little Scotsman who really came alive behind the wheel. Car and driver moving as one creature, sensing the road and reacting half a second before any other drivers even noticed the stimulus. All this, and not a single disturbance to my pile of crappy hatemongering.

Part two of the file was a lot less crappy than the first part. More eloquent, for a start, and a lot more reasonable-sounding. Someone with an IQ had written this, and probably a decent degree: the language was couched more softly, as if the author wanted to sidle up beside you and say the things you were already thinking, then take you on to a place you hadn't realised you were going. It's one thing to admit that housing is a problem in modern Britain, but another to say that the solution is an end to immigration, accompanied by forced repatriations – this was the kind of writing that made the latter sound like a good idea, a *reasonable* idea, the kind of idea that reasonable people already had but were afraid to admit in a world gone mad with political correctness. It was all bullshit, of course – spend five minutes in some of the places these immigrants come from and you'll realise why they wanted out badly enough to dodge militias, death squads and marauding gangs of heavily armed loonies.

But it was still perfectly normal as far as the boys and girls at Thames House were concerned, and thus a total waste of my time. I'd cancelled a studio session for this, and even though it was for a bunch of talentless 80s hacks trying to cash in on the comeback craze it was still better than reading bullshit in the back of a car on the M4. The file was running out fast, and so was my patience.

Thankfully, things got a little more interesting five pages before the end. We were into handwritten territory now, scrawled numbers and symbols that looked a lot more like my kind of candy. It appeared that the original owner of these papers had an interest in my very particular line of spookery, judging by the runes, astrological notation and calculations here. This was definitely worth my time, and I started photographing the pages. This was going to need more work than I had time for, and I'd have sooner kept the originals if there was any choice in the matter.

In fact, why not? The idea of giving me the originals to look at was so I could get a feel for the hand behind them, since photocopies only do you so much good when it comes to this kind of thing. Those were undoubtedly already back at the office undergoing whatever the backroom boys could think of. Cheltenham wouldn't get that much benefit from the originals, anyway.

A few sheets of paper and a biro were easy enough to find, so I had the driver pull into the services at Bristol and started copying out the scrawls well enough to fool someone who didn't plan to use them for what I had in mind. It took the best part of an hour, including a couple of breaks when my eyes started to go funny. When that happened I looked out at the view of Bristol, and thought of my last visit there, and the clusterfuck that had come in its wake. I'd have to make time to visit Annie – Sophie – and Geoff; it had been too long.

The guilt trip faded as we drove up the M5 towards Cheltenham. I was in the front of the car now, with the file back in its folder and comfortably locked into a briefcase resting on my lap. The handcuff attaching said luggage to my wrist was a nice touch, I thought, even if it did chafe a bit.

Passing through the outer gates of GCHQ was easy enough – a suitable ID had been left in the glove compartment and it took me cheerfully into the secure reception area where I was met by a friendly enough bloke from the Black Country who described himself as a deputy section head. The room was pretty much like any other government building, only with flasher coffee mugs – some kind of red and blue swooping design had replaced the old ones with the crest on. I liked the old mugs better: they made you look like you worked for the government instead of some godsawful PR firm.

Briefcase handed over, and no questions asked, I returned to the car. We drove back to London in silence.

That night, I spent some deeply meaningful hours with the notes I'd snaffled. The style was old-fashioned, but a reconstructed system nonetheless – something most likely from a movement that claimed to be thousands of years old but was actually formed in the back of an old cheese shop somewhere in Europe during the late nineteenth century by someone with a few bits of papyrus and a convincing line in mystical bollocks. Judging by the use of runes, it was probably claiming to be northern European, veering towards Germany rather than Scandinavia. Of course, this would fit in with all the goose-stepping crap, which was something that confused me: if you're so big on national pride and all that nonsense, why use someone else's magic when there's perfectly good stuff at home? Mind you, I don't really expect sense from any type of extremist – that's part of the definition, after all.

Fortunately for me, there's an Internet, and for every extremist there's an opposite who wants to expose their evil to the world. I spent the night trawling through website after website, with breaks to cross-check stuff in my own library. This was interesting: nothing quite matched what I had in front of me. There were elements that worked, but while the whole collection of notes seemed to be coherent within its own system, I couldn't find any references to such a system in any of the usual places. It wasn't showing up in the *un*usual places, either. That meant it was likely to be from an unknown outfit, and that meant it was now very firmly in my domain – or at least that of the Service.

So that's what I told the Boss.

'We've got definite indications of magic use, although it looks like that's part of an inner framework outside of public sight. The system's apparent origins tie in too closely with the material to be ignored, and from what I can glean from the police reports, this guy wasn't smart enough to be doing it on his own. That indicates an organised group, which makes me think it's worth sending someone to have a look.'

'Agreed,' said the Boss. 'Infiltrate, evaluate and report back when there's something to tell. A cover's been set up, something respectable that will appeal to the higher-ups looking for nice, normal people rather than the thugs they use as muscle. How much do you know about banking?'

'They're slow to pay interest and quick to charge for a letter?' Jokes weren't exactly the Boss's forte, but what I knew about high finance could be written on the head of a pin – without need for a microdot.

'Then you've got some learning to do. Background.' The red folder travelling across the desk towards me wasn't exactly a surprise. After all, when you've got blond hair and blue eyes, there's not much guesswork required to work out who's off to talk to the Nazi Party.

Chapter Two

Learning about the banking industry was as boring as you'd expect it to be. A succession of very dull men explained the process of shares, stocks, bonds, treasury certificates, precious metals, commodities and foreign exchange over the following week, while I spent my nights reading even duller books on economic theory and condensed company reports that would allow me to sound as if I knew what I was talking about. I was expected to fool people who did this shit for a living, people who found it interesting – exciting, even – and I couldn't just hide in a corner since I'd need to build a social circle that would take me into the target's area of influence.

That area of influence started with a broker named Michael. GCHQ had intercepted some dodgy-looking emails from his personal account several months ago, and further investigation showed that while he seemed like a nice enough bloke to the outside world, his private opinions were a little less friendly. The decision had been made to leave him in place as an unwitting intelligence source, and the bugs in his flat had revealed that when he wasn't working his way through the back office, he was talking to some very antisocial people. It was thanks to him that we'd scooped up the bedsit in Camden, when the occupant had bragged about kicking some poor gay bloke to death while his boyfriend watched. New avenues of inquiry were discovered, and suddenly the Met had another arrest (and pretty much guaranteed conviction) on the scoreboard.

Boy, am I glad we don't have to report *our* arrest rate. It wouldn't make pretty reading.

Michael was a bit of a foodie, so the other thing I had to learn was cookery. This was more fun, since I've spent most of my life eating out of restaurants, takeaways, rat-packs and ready meals and there's only so much polystyrene a boy can eat. The idea was that I'd start by engaging his taste buds, then engage his mind and let him take me on to where I actually wanted to be. Apparently Chef was impressed by my appreciation of a sharp knife. I can't think why.

A month passed this way in total. I moved into the cover's flat quietly and without fuss, and practised farting around with sauces while I recited stock-market shorthand codes for a few hundred companies that were liable to be of interest in the day job. I poached fish while revising the mechanisms of international money transfers, and to make sure that my politics were sound I whipped up a fantastic crème brûlée to the speeches of John Tyndall and Oswald Mosley. That last rather spoiled my appetite, but everything has a downside in this business.

The upside was the wine. My tastes are pretty simple, to be honest – a pint of beer or the occasional bottle of Vino Collapso de Blanco if I'm eating in a restaurant. All that changed as I started to get my head around grapes, vineyards and vintages. Then there was beer in way more forms than I ever thought possible: there was as much to learn here as there was about wine. Frankly, the beer was more confusing by the time I'd gone through hops, malt and yeast, and the various permutations in which they could be put together. Going back to a pint of Wifebeater would be a bit of a challenge after this.

But the end result seemed pretty convincing. I could waffle on like a good 'un about the stock market, feign enthusiasm about people with more money in the bank than I'd ever see in a lifetime and produce the kind of meal that didn't make Chef want to hit me over the head with a pan. I even managed to stop burning the pans after a while, since until then I'd only ever really cooked with two levels of heat: Gas Mark Fires of Hell and Off.

Not so shabby, but one thing I'd wanted to test had been off-limits. Chef had made it very clear that if I tried throwing any of his knives at a target he'd be using me for a knife block very shortly afterwards. I'd have to make time to try that later.

There were other things to be done, as well: notably establishing a presence. The City is a village in some ways – if you don't know someone, you probably know someone who does. That meant establishing a few friends. First stop was finding a pub.

Pubs are great. They're instant social networking sites that make the Internet look like a cave painting. Make the right few friends, spin them a tale and the next thing you know you've got a reference. City pubs, however, are harder to break in to because the patrons tend to drink in packs. But there's a way around that as well . . .

Derek was the first point of contact. He didn't go out with the boys much, preferring a nice little local just off Blackfriars Road that was handy for his flat. He lived alone, having been divorced twice when his wives both decided that the money didn't make up for him being more interested in numbers than in them. He was also a little older than most of the guys in his department, which made him calmer and easier to talk to.

It took a couple of weeks, but making friends with the guy was easy enough once you broke through the barrier. He was lonely, and my cover of having just come out of the Army, studied and got through the broker licensing exams on my own was about right. He thought I was an idiot for picking the City as a new career, but didn't mind sharing a few stories of particularly intricate trades that filled out my knowledge base

21

very nicely indeed. He even started to let me know where there were jobs going, at his own bank and a few others, and when a junior trader post came up at Michael's bank I was all primed up and ready to ace the interview.

I've done a few job interviews over the years, as a number of different people, so I know what employers are looking for. The bank wanted someone who was enthusiastic, confident, willing to work like a carthorse and clearly focused on making a lot of money, so that's what I gave them. I threw in a touch of ruthlessness and a side order of aggression to round it out, and backed it all up with a bit of charm so I came off as a *likeable* asshole rather than just another asshole.

Whether it was that or the charm I'd worked to give me an extra edge just before I went in didn't matter, I got the job. Good thing, too: I wouldn't have liked to explain to the Boss that the bastards wouldn't hire me. Two months of prep down the tubes would not have made him a happy boy.

The next hurdle was the first day at work. Through the overdecorated reception, up to HR, and then down to the trading floor. The whole building was almost completely devoted to trading, with people shouting into telephones, staring at screens full of data and swilling caffeine like there was no tomorrow. I knew that the banking industry had a high burnout rate, and I was starting to see why. I was introduced to my new boss and left to get on with it.

Harvey, my team leader, talked me through the displays at the desk I'd be sharing with him while I found my feet. I'd read up on them beforehand, but kept it quiet so I'd look like a quick learner. I needed to start making an impression pretty quickly, and this was one of the methods I'd picked. The other had needed some assistance from the folks back home, but I figured it was worth the effort and would give me an in long enough to catch up on my own merits.

The rest of the day went just as you'd expect, as did the rest of the week. There were the obligatory welcome drinks, where I got to meet Michael for the first time as well as the rest of the team. He seemed reasonably likeable, and kept his politics under wraps. I dropped a couple of hints but left it there, since we mostly talked about wine – well, he did most of the talking, and it was about how much he spent on wine, but I managed to slip in a couple of hints that I might have an idea of what he was talking about. It was a start, anyway.

After a week, I was allowed to start making trades and building a portfolio of clients. This was where some of the outside help came in, since most of the clients had already been arranged by the Service using a network of false identities, shell companies and professional middlemen. I even managed to snag some cash from my American friend Brutus, on the understanding that I promised to turn him a profit. By the end of the second week I had a few million to play with, most of it taxpayers' money, and was starting to get a bit of a reputation for being a good 'closer'.

Week three had the first part of the next phase, and another fix. A small technology company announced a new product, and the share price went from peanuts to pricey in about twenty minutes. A little industrial espionage had yielded that closely guarded secret a week early, and I'd been moving money into them slowly enough not to make a dent in the price before the announcement. By the end of the day I'd made the best part of a million quid, and got a bottle of champagne for my trouble. That attracted Michael's attention faster than any amount of wine blather, and from there we got to the subject of a game of squash.

I hate squash. It's a stupid game that consists of hitting a ball against a wall and a load of macho gloating, but the exercise was good for me. Michael's club was in one of those overpriced designer gyms I hate even more than the game we were playing, another example of 'lifestyle' gone mad. I didn't have to let him beat me – it's not as if I play a lot and it was obvious that he did.

'Never mind, mate, you can't win at everything.' It was the first time that Michael had said anything more than how great he was, and hopefully meant I was getting inside the armour that very clearly separated his work and private lives. I made a show of buying him dinner for beating me on the promise of a rematch and let him talk work, women and wine for the evening. Eventually we got round to a bit of politics, and that's where he throttled back a little. It was obvious to me that he was sounding me out, pushing me in certain directions and seeing how far I was willing to go. Neither of us got anywhere near deporting every foreigner in the country, but there was an element of comparing how some immigrants contribute more than others and how certain parts of society would benefit from a little pruning. Nothing overt there, but a lot of the insidious crap that extremists use to get under your skin. The idea that I was dealing with a nasty piece of work got a little more reinforcement when we switched topics to women. Michael was not what I'd call discreet about his conquests, and obviously enjoyed bragging about the women at work he'd bedded as well as those he'd met through other circumstances. He didn't exactly come across as a considerate lover either, more focused on his score than whether or not there had been any repeat engagements. On the upside, he clued me in to which of the women at his gym might be interested in a little dalliance – something else to help establish my identity as an asshole.

We parted on much better terms than we'd started the evening. It looked as if I'd made the right impression, and had room to keep the work going.

And when the work was done, I was going to really enjoy killing that fucker.

Chapter Three

Another month passed. More fixed deals sent my star into the ascendant and a few extra clients started coming my way in the more conventional manner, supplemented by another stack from the Treasury. God only knows what they thought they were putting money into, but that kind of cover isn't my problem and there wasn't much danger of it going away anytime soon – there were more rigged deals to come. Added to that was the fact that I was getting the hang of things and making trades the usual way in a reasonably profitable manner. Brutus sent me a note thanking me for doubling his money, and to let me know that he'd taken back his original stake so there would be no hard feelings if anything went wrong (although he expected a warning if I had one to give).

As my position at the bank was established, so was my friendship with Michael. More squash, more meals and a few reported conquests did me no harm in his eyes, and a tip I slipped him made his balance sheet look very good one afternoon. When he started to wonder where I was getting my information, I hinted that Army mates get everywhere, and a lot of them help each other out occasionally.

This was the hook. A comment like this reported to the wrong people could turn into an investigation into insider trading, and it was a gamble for me to tell him such a naughty secret. He liked the fact that I'd just given him a fairly major bit of dirt on me, and had the good sense not to show it. My bet was that he had his own agenda anyway, and a bit of insurance would help him advance it.

Which is exactly what happened. Our next trip to the pub included a man named Martin who was supposedly from Michael's martial arts group. The group had been mentioned a couple of times, and various styles of fighting had been discussed as part of our macho bonding bullshit, but this was an obvious step forward for it to come out into the open. Where Michael was an effusive host, fond of grand gestures, Martin was tighter: tighter lipped, tighter built and obviously tighter on security. We talked about the Army a bit – he'd been in for a while before getting thrown out for sticking a recruit's head down the toilet once too often – and I must have done a good enough job of convincing him for the conversation to get back onto politics by the time we arrived at Michael's flat. Without the world watching, views slowly drifted further and further to the right. I quoted a few bits of the extremist stuff I'd read, which went down a treat, and followed it up by pushing them to say a little more. Once I got them onto the subject of secrecy, Michael was happy to lead the conversation right where I wanted it to go.

'I mean, it's not like we're saying things that people aren't thinking, is it?' The booze was cutting in and he was obviously on a favourite topic. 'It's just that you can't say it openly without getting labelled a racist!' There were sounds of assent, which he took as a cue to continue. 'I mean, I love my country. What's wrong with that? All I want is what's best for everybody, and if that means being more careful about immigration or sending a few people who don't like the way it is here back home, what's the problem? Look at Willem, the Dutch guy – he made us a packet last year, and he's an immigrant. What I'm on about are the ones who come here just to claim benefits. That's my fucking taxes they're stealing, and what do we get for it? A load of crap about how our natural way of life isn't to their liking and how it should be messed around with until it is. Well, fuck that. Send the fuckers back home and save us money as well as grief.'

Exactly what I wanted to hear. With the nut cracked, we started dissecting political correctness, racial equality and political asylum late into the night. It was nearly dawn as I got out of the cab at my flat, happy that some real progress was finally being made. Job satisfaction's a weird thing in my line of business, and while I felt like I needed a shower after all that, I was smiling when I stepped under the water.

My little performance seemed to work for Michael and Martin, too. Michael caught me at the bank after the weekend to let me know that I'd been invited to train with their martial arts club that Wednesday evening. They thought I'd fit in.

The club met in a little gym in the East End, the sort of place where nobody asked questions or paid too much attention to who turned up. It was grotty in the way that only a real gym can be, and the boxing ring on the ground floor looked well used. We were upstairs, in a large open room. No mats on the ground, so I'd have to make sure that my breakfalls were right or I might get hurt. The lighting was harsh, and the whitewashed walls slightly short of what I'd call clean. Given the company I was expecting, this seemed more than a little fitting.

There were fourteen of them in total. A collection of specimens that would, in the main, look pretty much at home in a pub brawl or football riot. Michael didn't look as if he fitted in all that well, and Martin was like a social bridge between him and the rest of the group. Then there was the obvious instructor, a man named Graeme. Just shy of six feet, he was a wiry-looking bastard with dark hair and a goatee beard. He'd been sizing me up since I'd walked into the room.

'I hear you used to be in the Army.' Obviously, words like hello were considered extraneous around here.

'For a bit, yeah.' It seemed better to play his game.

'Right. How's your unarmed combat?'

'Pretty rusty. It's been a wh—' His fist seemed to come out of nowhere, and I was reacting almost before I saw his shoulders move. By the time it was where I'd been standing I was a foot away, braced into a stance and ready to continue the discussion.

'Not that rusty, I'd say!' Graeme laughed, and the class laughed with him. 'That's the first rule, you lot: always be ready.' There were various sounds of agreement. 'This is a sparring class, John. Feel up to it?' He was talking to me. I was, for the moment, John Dennis.

'Sure.'

The night consisted mainly of handy brawlers having a go at each other in rotation, with me just thrown into the mix. I held back a bit, not wanting to stand out but still keeping my game high enough to not get hurt. A couple of hours of this, and people were starting to get tired. Personally, I was enjoying myself and ready for more.

'Right, John,' said Graeme, 'not a bad showing. Before we go for a pint, there's one tradition we have for new members. Ready?' Again, the first move was supposed to be a surprise. One of the thugs came from behind my left shoulder swinging a right hook that was meant for the back of my head. Duck to let it go by, pop up under his shoulder, snake an arm around him, lift and dump on the floor – not too hard, since this was supposedly friendly. As I moved away, another came in from the direction I was moving. Twist around him, trip him up and watch him fall. Perfect.

The fist in my right kidney came as a bit of a surprise, as did the fact that it was obviously at full power – I was going to be pissing blood in the morning by the feel of that. Graeme had taken advantage of my diverted attention to get in behind me. I spun round, my right elbow at face height to keep him busy while my left fist went looking for his solar plexus. He took them both on his guard and stepped away. Martin was next, so I reversed my spin, kicked his knee out and hit him hard enough to crack a rib or two. Time to ramp things up a bit.

There's an old saying: you don't win a fight with multiple targets, you merely survive. I'd only survived this long because they were coming at me one by one, giving me time to deal with one before the next appeared. This was good news, since if they'd really wanted to mess me up they'd have come in groups. Too many would have got in each other's way, but three or four would have been plenty to take care of business.

The next one got thrown straight into two more of his mates, knocking them flat on their backsides. As far as I could tell the rules were that if you were down you were out, and everything else went. No problem, then – I didn't have to seriously injure everyone.

Michael was on his way in now, and I couldn't help having a laugh at his expense. One punch turned his nose from three dimensions to two, and he sat back on his arse bleeding like a stuck pig. That felt *good*.

Halfway through, and the really tough guys were coming out to play. Another duck and shove put the next one down, along with the guy he collided with. The next went into the wall as I avoided his charge – possibly the second broken nose of the evening, but this time the victim didn't look as if he was a stranger to the experience.

The last four came in at once. I charged the first one, knocking him down and treading on his guts as I broke out of the box they were trying to trap me in. A foot hit the back of my knee and I sank down. As they came in for the kill I caught one with a karate chop between the legs. He didn't go down, but after I did it again he seemed to lose all interest in the fight.

The fist that took me arrived then, straight into the back of my head as the other survivor kicked me in the ribs. I'm tough, but there are limits – and right then the floor looked pretty inviting. Down I went.

I think that extra kick in the ribs might have been cheating, but it seemed a bit churlish to say anything.

Graeme was laughing and applauding. 'I thought I was going to have to finish you off myself for a minute there! Nice work, John.' The people who'd just been trying to knock seven shades of shit out of me were now helping me to my feet, clapping me on the back and making sounds of welcome – quite a contrast to the guarded attitude I'd been getting up till now. It seemed that they had decided I was tough enough to join their little gang.

Once we'd cleaned up and dressed a few sore bits, it was time for beer. Graeme led us down the road to an equally grotty pub decked out with Union flags and posters that didn't exactly speak of universal love. The barmaid seemed unfazed by all of this, although it looked more like she was too stupid to realise what sort of place she was working in than she was going to pull out a Nazi Party membership card.

They were drinking cheap and nasty lager, so I went for scotch. That educational month had definitely had an effect, and the cheap whisky was a better option than the muck that most of the group were consuming – especially after I'd hidden it behind a load of ginger ale. I noticed that Michael had taken courage from my refusal to stick with the herd and joined me on the Loch Turpentine.

Conversation was pretty much what you'd expect from a bunch of meatheads: cars, sex and football. Of course, most conversations about football tend to be more focused on the game than the fighting afterwards, but those members of the group who indulged took a perverse pride in their engagements, like warriors comparing battles a thousand years ago. Beowulf and Grendel might sound more noble, but it's still the tale of a bunch of hard men going round to beat up someone who's giving their mate a bit of trouble. Point is, violence is violence, and the only real difference between me and the people talking was the causes for which we showed up. Hating one bunch of people turned into hating other bunches of people: gays, foreigners, anyone who was different from them got a slice of the action. The amount of anger these people were carrying was amazing, and somehow I managed to slot right in, channelling the dislike I was feeling for them into the targets they picked. I was nowhere near as bad as some of them but it seemed to be the right kind of pitch to let them accept me as one of the gang. We finished with a bunch of them deciding that I was coming back next week and away we went into the night.

As we made our way west, Michael was excitable. I got the feeling that he'd had trouble fitting in with some of the group, and bringing me along had raised their opinion of him. I wasn't surprised: Michael was clearly out of his weight class with this lot, despite his opinions gelling with theirs. I decided to push his good mood a little and see what it got me.

'Aren't this mob a bit, you know, below your class? Salt of the earth and all that, but a bit, well, not quite your type?' Michael's obvious weak point was his vanity, and playing him up felt like the right way to go. It was.

'Oh, they're a decent enough bunch. No point turning my back on where I came from just 'cause I've made a few quid. But yeah, there's another bunch I know. A bit more up-market. Trouble is, I can't really invite you along to that one myself. Let me have a word with a few people and see what happens, eh? You seemed happy enough, though. My bloody nose hurts like hell.'

'You tried to hurt me, but I hurt you first. Just tell the drones it's a squash injury.' He hadn't had a prayer, but it wouldn't have done me any good to underline the point. Somewhere deep inside he already knew it.

'That's the tradition: if you can't take a bit of rough and tumble, there's no point you coming back. I got worse than that my first night when Martin took me along. Bloody hell, I thought Graeme was going to pile in there for a minute and you really don't want to mess with him.' He leaned closer. 'Used to be in the SAS, they say. Thrown out for overdoing it a bit in Northern Ireland.'

'Oh yeah?' Just like Martin, then. I made a note to see what I could find out. There seemed to be a pattern here, and it looked like my chosen cover was an even better move than I'd imagined.

I got home, swept the place for anything that might have been planted while I was out and started typing up my report on the laptop I kept in the false bottom of the wardrobe. It was about time I sent some news home. Descriptions, names, places, everything that had happened that night, along with a request for anything that could be found on Martin and Graeme. The other lads might have been a bit on the dim side, but there was a lot more going on with those two than nasty comments in the pub and a bit of fisticuffs in a backstreet gym. They'd enjoyed dealing out the violence just a little too much for my liking, and I was willing to bet that they weren't just doing it in the gym.

The other thing I was willing to bet was that I had their attention.

Chapter Four

It took a couple of days for an answer to come back from the Boss, since my set-up for communications was disjointed by necessity. I had to assume that I was being watched from my first conversation with Derek back in Blackfriars, so things went something like this:

I'd established a pattern of going for a five-mile run each morning. It was a good way of keeping in shape and, thanks to the routes I'd picked, a good way of checking if I was being followed. Varying the route and time of my run made sure that I'd notice if the same faces kept cropping up. If I wanted to drop something off, I'd leave my bedroom curtains in a particular fashion, stick an encrypted USB key inside my shorts and take the route that passed a particular public toilet. On the way past, I'd stop for a comfort break and hide the key in a hollowed-out tile inside one of the stalls. A piece of piss, if you'll forgive the pun. If the Boss had a message for me, then a particular car would be parked in a particular spot, and there'd be a van waiting for me as I came around the corner on my opening stretch. My MP3 player, carefully chosen for its wireless Internet capability and given a small software hack by one of the tame geeks, would pick up a burst transmission and turn it into an audio file that played once and then erased itself. This way I'd get the message while I was running and any data that might come with it would be disguised as a piece of music until it went through the laptop, and nobody knew who they were talking to – at least in theory.

Don't knock it – it works.

That morning had found a battered old hatchback parked on the street outside, marked with a sticker that read 'Neighbourhood Witch'. Someone had a sense of humour, but it meant that I was to pack my brain and be ready for something to listen to.

'We've found your martial arts friends,' said a very friendly-sounding female voice through the headphones. 'Martin Gibson and Graeme Flory. Gibson was discharged quietly for abusing recruits at the training facility where he was stationed, and Flory went for nearly killing someone in a fight over a woman. No sign that he was in the SAS, although we have a note that his application was rejected because of his overly aggressive nature. He's not listed as having been to Northern Ireland either, since he was in Colchester at the time. He does have a criminal record, though: several charges of assault, all dropped when the witnesses decided not to testify. Judging by the sound of his friends, I don't think that comes as too much of a surprise. We tracked his Internet usage, and he's been visiting several extremist websites; his anonymiser isn't anywhere near as good as he thinks it is. There's also been some activity researching various establishments in Soho that don't fit the profile of the sort of place he'd be likely to go: several gay bars that are popular on the scene and a couple of club nights. It's sufficiently out of his pattern that we thought it was worth mentioning, so see what else you can find out.

'Gibson also has a record for violence, but he seems cleverer at covering his tracks. We think he might be the actual brains of the operation, and using Flory to draw attention by playing the faithful acolyte in public. He's been mentioned in more than one murder investigation and has links, albeit tenuous ones, to a couple of people that Special Branch have an interest in. Be aware that following him up too closely might bring you to police attention and that this is something we'd prefer to avoid at the present time. Use your discretion, and good luck. Message ends.'

ZZ Top flowed back into the space left by the sexy voice. It was computer-generated, I knew that, but it didn't stop me from putting an image to it, one that was tight-laced on the outside but wild underneath. Ah, the ways you pass the time when you're running.

I'd have to wait until I was pulled in to make the next move, since pushing any harder would spook them. Michael became my new best friend, proud of the broken nose I'd given him as if it was some kind of badge even as he fed everyone else the bullshit about squash I'd suggested. It might have been, for him – some people get trapped in pointless lives and forget that meaning comes from within, so they fall into the trap of being defined by what others think, their possessions, their job, or something equally shallow. I suppose that's an advantage I have, in a way: a fluid identity means that I have to know myself inside it all, or be swallowed by my covers to the point where I lose all sense of self and become even more hollow than the people around me.

So I worked the profile, massaged Michael's ego, got a bit beaten up once a week and sang nasty songs in the pub afterwards. A lot of the martial arts guys were starting to respect me now, impressed by the fact that I managed to be tough and smart at the same time. It was obvious that they'd seen Michael as a bit of a joke, but there was none of that with me. In fact, I could see something brewing among them that would probably come in handy as long as I let it come to fruition naturally. I showed them a couple of useful tricks, too, letting them see a willingness to contribute to the group in exchange for the welcome they'd given me. Basic anthropology, but when you're dealing with apes you don't need to try too hard. Martin and Graeme, however, were a different matter. They had also noticed the respect I was accruing and I got the definite impression that it was weighing in my favour as a decision was made about my future.

After the fourth session, one of the thugs invited me along for another beer after the traditional session in the pub. His name was Gary, a bricklayer and part-time football hooligan, and he thought I might like to come along with some of the lads for a bit of a late one at this pub he knew. It was either a breakthrough or a trap, and I pretty much had to hope it was the former while preparing for the latter. Michael looked heartbroken as he headed off to the Tube alone, but that was his tough luck. He wasn't one of these people no matter how much he wanted to be, and I could see that he was being used by Graeme and Martin for reasons unclear – probably financial, since the money to rent the gym had to come from somewhere and nobody had mentioned paying any kind of subscription.

I bimbled off with Gary and the lads in the direction of a somewhat more fashionable area of the East End, ending up about a hundred yards from where the new money was making its inroads to the places where families had been living for generations. The pub we were in paid no mind to that – it was clear that if you had new money you weren't welcome. Nicotine-stained walls; an old, pitted bar counter that must have come from the sixties, at least; ashtrays branded with cheap lagers and piled with dog-ends as though the smoking ban had yet to happen: it was like stepping back in time, and if you'd told the fashionable people they'd have been on it like a plague of locusts, talking about authentic charm and proper characters. The simple response to this when someone of that type walked in was to refuse them service, then offer violence if they tried to make a fuss. It seemed to work, too, since I saw one group of bright young things bounced without anyone batting an eyelid. This was a *proper* boozer, and no mistake.

Conversation here was along much the same lines as before,

only with a more aggressive edge. They were working themselves up on a combination of adrenalin and cheap booze, obviously getting ready to do something. As soon as someone mentioned a gay club around the corner I could see where it was going – and it wasn't somewhere I liked the idea of. But this job isn't designed for consciences. It's about getting shit done, and when the party got to its feet, I went with them.

The couple we found were harmless enough, just kissing in a side street. In many ways it was a really stupid thing for them to be doing, but it didn't deserve what was coming. Someone handed me a black balaclava, which I slipped over my head almost without thinking.

'What we got 'ere, then?' It was Gary who spoke, obviously leader of this little group and presumably wanting to impress me. 'A couple of fairies doing the nasty? You make me fucking sick!' I could see the fear this little speech had caused, and rather than running, the couple froze long enough for us to surround them. Then it began. The whole thing was pretty run-of-the-mill technically, nothing to mark it out from any other kicking I've given over the years other than the number of people I was doing it with. The looks of terror on our victims was the same, the pleading for mercy, the ruthless efficiency with which I placed boot and fist, the blood on the pavement . . .

It was just the wrong reason to hand out a beating.

We went back to the same pub afterwards, since they appeared to have the same fairly casual attitude to opening hours that they had to a crafty fag with your pint. Spirits were high, and I faked a matching mood. There was much clapping on the back for me, since I was now a fully fledged member of their pack. I bought a round to celebrate, laughed and joked about what we'd done the way no professional ever would and gave the impression of a very happy drunk who'd just had a liberating experience. I let them think that I'd wanted to do it for ages, but not had the guts to – an admission that really impressed them, since it let them think that they'd helped me come out of my shell a bit. I turned down an invitation to join them at a football game the following Saturday, pleading too many cameras and not being able to afford the risk to my job. Then it was time to take a cab home, snatch an hour's sleep and head back to work as though this was a normal day for me.

Michael asked what we'd done after he left, and I told him he didn't want to know, with a sly wink and a hint that he'd get a clue if he read the newspapers. It was there in the *Standard*, all right: 'COUPLE BEATEN OUTSIDE NIGHTCLUB'. One was in intensive care and it was going to be a long time before the other one got the smile back that he had in this photograph. They looked like good kids, and my memory flashed on the way they'd been kissing: tender, like a couple rather than a one-night stand. Part of me felt sick to my stomach, but it was the part locked away deep underneath my cover, which was suppressing a satisfied smile. Michael's eyes were wide at the idea that someone he thought he knew well was actually doing the things he wished he could.

As a gesture of solidarity, I took him to the pub that night, then we ended up back at my place. I wanted him to get a look at the bookshelf, and cooking backed up with a decent scotch seemed like a good reason to do it. The books were a plant, obviously. Among the cookery books and fashionable novels for reading as I commuted were a few well-chosen biographies, political works from the far right and a small selection of low-level occult stuff. We ate an omelette that Chef might actually have considered acceptable, drank half a bottle of Scotland's finest and made conversation about a range of subjects, but he just kept coming back to the previous night's beating. He wanted to know how it felt, what it was like to show these people that their perverted bullshit wasn't acceptable in a decent society. I fed him all the right noises while carefully not admitting to anything and sent him away happy. I hadn't had much time for him before, but now he was right down there with the rest of the sewer rats.

After another Friday at work, I was wiped. I needed something to get my head back into a shape approaching normal before I started getting sucked into this bullshit for real. I needed a friend. There were a few really dumb choices for this, which cut out most of my real-life social grouping, and only a couple of people I could trust to keep their mouths shut. Brutus was out of the country doing something I was glad to know nothing about, which left me sitting on a train to North London watching my back for tails as I held on to a carrier bag containing a bottle of gin, a bottle of tonic, a bottle of very nice single malt and three plastic cups.

Looking around to make sure I was clear, then through the hole in the fence left by some helpful young people. The dark and silent walk through the grass, watching out for obstacles human, stone and otherwise, and finally coming to the covered walkway that made a good spot to meet. I got out the cups, poured two measures of scotch and a gin and tonic, then sat back against the stone with one of the former.

'You look like shit, Jack.'

'Feel like it, too. There's a drink over there for you.' I pointed at the two plastic cups that I'd set up nearby.

'Ta. You undercover again?'

'Just a bit. Working through a bunch of scumbag right-wingers and waiting for the grown-ups to make contact.'

'I thought you liked that sort of thing?' A new voice, female. Someone who'd been in the same position I was now. I could only hope that when I needed my backup, he'd be better than hers had been.

'I'm good at it, Sophie. That doesn't mean I like it. These

fuckers are just plain nasty, and they're only an adjunct to the people I'm going after.'

'Oh.' Sophie thought about this as she inhaled her G&T. Dead Geoff (and I hope I don't need to explain why I call him Dead Geoff) looked me over with eyes that had seen the Other Side in far more detail than I fancied thinking about.

'This one getting to you, is it, Jack? Is the man of ice melting a bit?'

'Not melting, no. I just don't get off on beating up innocent people.'

'There's an argument that—' Geoff's look silenced Sophie before she could finish the sentence. She was too soft to have been put in the field, and looking back on it I was amazed that she could stand the sight of me after the job we'd worked together.

'There's a way you deal with this, Sophie: there are Good Guys – that's us, and there are Bad Guys, like this bunch of shitbag hooligans. One side against the other is fair – we go after them and vice versa. Civilians getting caught in the crossfire isn't supposed to happen.' I was becoming angry, not so much with Sophie's naivety but with the situation I was in. I had the horrible feeling that I was going to have to go out with Gary again, and the prospect wasn't one that filled me with joy.

'What's the count?' Geoff brought me back to business, getting me to talk it through so I could go back to work. His time in the field may have run out, but he was still my best mate.

'Two so far, with a high likelihood of more to come. Bad ones, too. Further than I'd have wanted to go with a beating.'

'Not killed?'

'No. One in ICU, the other just seriously fucked up.'

'Then they'll live. Could be worse.' Geoff made the weird noise that served him as laughter. 'They could be stuck here with Little Miss Starchyknickers.' Sophie looked horrified. Obviously they'd been getting along, and Geoff's distinctive personality was asserting itself with all his usual charm. 'Seriously, mate – you know the score. A couple of injured blokes versus possible body counts, chaos, mayhem and all that shit. Sacrifice a few to save the many.'

'Yeah.' I sighed. 'Doesn't mean I have to like it.'

'When you start liking it, mate, it's time to quit.'

'What are they like?' Sophie picked up the baton very nicely, getting me back to talking about the gig itself. Philosophy wasn't going to help me here; I just needed to spill to someone who gave a damn.

'They're pretty bad. Maybe as bad as the Sisterhood.'

'Shit.' It was just a whisper, but she meant it. The memories were still fresh and obviously her empathy was working full tilt.

'Yeah. Don't worry, I'll be all right. Line 'em up and take 'em out. Business as usual.'

'Right.' Geoff's last word on the subject, it seemed. We switched topics and talked about the outside world, scandals, who'd been caught with their hands in whose trousers and what was happening with the government. We talked about the old days, too, when Geoff still had a pulse and the two of us would occasionally go somewhere completely obscure and get outrageously drunk together. Sophie seemed both shocked and completely surprised by the sort of things we got up to, and flatly refused to believe the tale about how we almost stole a Royal Navy ship. Admittedly it was only a minesweeper, but I'm still willing to bet we would have got away with it if we'd been able to walk in a straight line at the time. It would certainly have given the Boss a headache trying to cover it up.

It was late, and I was knackered by about four. The Goths were changing shifts as couples shagging after the pub got their clothes back on and the ones who'd been clubbing snuck in to find a quiet spot. I decided to leave Dead Geoff to it, and let Sophie nag him about respecting people's privacy.

Chapter Five

Everything was going pretty much as planned. A slow infiltration works better than a fast one, and it helps when you give the people you're getting close to something that they think can be used as ammunition against you. By this point my nasty new friends thought they had me for insider dealing and assault, and this was exactly the sort of thing I wanted them to think. When somebody believes they've got something on you, they're liable to use it to drag you further in, to make you step over another, worse line so you're even more screwed if they decide to offer you up. Of course, you know what they're up to as well, so it works as a kind of mutual insurance policy. You don't drop them in it, they extend you the same courtesy – but if you get cold feet and want to blab, you'll be just as much in the shit as them, so everybody just keeps quiet and everything's hunky-dory.

Truth be told, given that it was only three months since I'd started at the bank I was doing pretty well. This was the part where I had to wait, fit in and let the target come to me. I kept going to the martial arts club, beat up a few more undeserving people because of their race or sexual preference and generally acted like the kind of asshole I was supposed to be. Patience was the key. The bad guys, meanwhile, had pulled my military records and started running checks on me to see how the data matched my story. They'd even gone so far as to send out a few feelers to see if they could find anyone I'd served with, which was a smart touch, but we'd thought of that and had a few people planted to give just the right impression. I'd got their attention, given them what they wanted and let them think that I could be a good recruit for the cause.

After four months of waiting, the next break came.

I was just about to leave the club with Gary and co when Graeme tapped me on the shoulder.

'Stick around, will you, John? We'd like a word.'

Everyone else drifted off, with poor old Michael shuffling away alone as always. I was starting to really feel sorry for Michael. Despite me having made an effort to integrate him with the rest of the group, his only real human contact was at the club – and when we occasionally hit a restaurant or cooked together. In fact, I'd somehow managed to become his best friend within this horrid little world and I was wondering if he might have started thinking about giving it all up if I hadn't been there.

We watched the last of the lads disappear around the corner, then Graeme and Martin led me back inside.

'What would you say if I told you that we had a little something extra going on at the moment, and thought you might be interested?' Graeme's tone was unconcerned, but he was watching me like a hawk, as was Martin.

'Depends on what it is, I suppose.' Not too eager, but open to the possibilities. A safe reply to start with.

'I hear you've been having a bit of fun with Gary, on his little hunting trips. Enjoy it, did you?'

'Once I'd got the blood off my boots, yeah. I don't want to think what I might catch from that if I didn't clean up properly, but it's about time someone explained what is and isn't acceptable in a decent society.'

'And you think that this is a decent society?'

'Is it bollocks!' I snorted a laugh. 'Perverts running around like they own the place, every lazy wog in the world coming here to sponge benefits and a government that thinks it's all right to let them do just that? Do me a favour. We're being sold out by our own people – liberals who think that some foreign bastard should have more rights than the people who live here already. Screw that.'

'I know exactly what you mean,' said Graeme, 'and we have a little idea that might send that message a touch more clearly than just beating up a random loser once a month or so.' Graeme looked to Martin, who nodded for him to continue. 'You've worked with explosives, right?'

'Once or twice, yeah.'

'Then we might have a little job for you to help out with, assuming you can keep your gob shut.'

I didn't even credit that with an answer, just raised an eyebrow and made a face that said everything a comment like that deserved.

'Right, then.' It was Martin, chipping in for the first time as he handed me a piece of paper. 'Here's a list of things we'd like you to pick up. Keep them at your place for the moment, and we'll arrange collection.'

'We appreciate your help, John.' Graeme's face had that scary look on it, the look of a True Believer. 'This is the sort of thing that makes a real difference, you know? We'll show these fuckers exactly what we think of them.'

'Right.' There wasn't a lot for me to say, really. I put the list in my pocket and went straight home.

What they wanted was obviously only part of the order. I'd been tasked to pick up a couple of common household chemicals, an electronic alarm clock and a packet of wire. Nothing that would generate suspicion on its own, but together with a few other bits and pieces I could see exactly what they were aiming for: plastic explosive and a detonator. Using the quantities on my list, I guessed that they were looking at a small device, something portable that could be left in a public place without causing too much attention. A briefcase or small backpack, most likely. But with a decent explosive, that would be more than enough to get someone's attention. A pub's worth easily, when I thought back to the report on Graeme's internet activity.

This would never do. Obviously I was going to have to do something about it, since I have an allergic reaction to bombs going off in my vicinity, and don't think much of people like Graeme and Martin playing around with them at all. There wasn't any profit in reporting it immediately, though, since I was prepared to bet that I was now being watched very carefully indeed. Besides, I didn't have much to tell yet – it's all very well saying that someone's planning a bombing, but that's not much good without a time and a target. Better to do as I'd been told, show that I could be trusted and hope to find out more. So over the next few days I went shopping.

They let me stew for a couple of weeks, while I carefully didn't say a word about the plan to anyone, including Martin and Graeme, even when I thought it might be safe to do so. They wanted to see whether I could keep my head, so that was what I showed them. Part of me was burning with curiosity, wanting to know everything so that I'd be able to report in and get the counter-plan under way, but I had no choice but to lock that down and keep on behaving like a good little storm-trooper.

Eventually I got a call from Martin, telling me that he'd be around that evening. We loaded everything into the back of his car, and as I stepped back to let him go he gave me a cold look.

'Where do you think you're going?'

'I've done my bit.'

'Not quite, John. Get in the car.'

I did as I was told, and Martin drove us to an industrial unit near Wimbledon surrounded by car repair outfits and a block of offices across the road. It was late, and the place was deserted. A door opened and then closed behind us as Martin drove the car inside. Only when the door was firmly closed did the lights come on. Graeme was waiting for us, with another man I hadn't seen before. This new character was obviously the man in charge: his body language made that very clear, as did Graeme's. He held his hand out to me as I got out of the car.

'You must be John. Glad to have you with us – I've heard a lot of good things about you.'

'Thank you.' I shook his hand and got an impression of strength in the grip. He had muscle under that shirt, which sat comfortably with the aura of command. Definitely ex-forces, and definitely an officer. His hair was cropped short and neatly styled. He could have still been in, but I doubted it somehow. It suddenly became a lot clearer how the group had pulled my fake Army record so easily, given that I was clearly dealing with someone a step further up the food chain.

'You can call me Mr White for the moment. I'm here to help get everything ready.'

'Right.' And with that, I seemed to be arse-deep in a bombing. We unloaded the car, moving my shopping to a large bench that already held the other items I was expecting to see: a few more chemical products, soldering gear and a large plastic bucket for mixing things together. I ended up helping Mr White with his little chemistry lesson, handing him things as he asked for them and watching to see if I could identify his technique, which was disturbingly similar to my own. After a couple of very careful hours we had four lumps of plastic explosive, each about the size of a house brick.

'Think you could do it on your own now, John?' Mr White's tone was friendly, a sign that our time together had gone well so far, I thought.

'Not yet, but show me again and I might be willing to have a go.'

'Good answer. Overconfidence will kill you with this sort of thing. Better to go as slow as you and avoid the risk wherever possible.' He was starting to sound disturbingly like the people who'd taught me to do this back in training, the same relaxed manner communicating the deadly serious lessons of explosives safety. 'If we repeat the exercise, John, I might just have a chance to show you properly. As it is, time is of the essence and I have to construct a detonator. If you'll excuse me?' He turned to face the electronics at the end of the bench before I had a chance to reply – I was obviously dismissed.

At the other table, Graeme and Martin were looking at the floor plan of what appeared to be a pub. There was a bar along one wall, tables at each end and a long shelf with stools opposite the bar where the building was too narrow for any other seating. Toilets were at the far end from the street entrance, and there was a side door on the long side opposite the utility room that sat next to the bar. Next to the plan sat a template indicating a blast cone, which signalled that they were looking for spots to place the device that Mr White was finishing. The choice of template was interesting, more like a Claymore mine than a regular bomb, showing more sophistication than was usual in attacks of this type. Of course, with all the military training in the room that was hardly a surprise.

'What do you think, John? Where would we get most damage?' Graeme was looking over my shoulder.

'Depends on the detonation method. If you want to get really sneaky, plant it at the back and have the guy with the trigger fire it from the Gents. He'll be safe, but processed with the victims afterwards and hopefully clear of suspicion.' I stopped to think for a second. 'It's not me, is it?'

'No, John, it's not you.'

'Right. Then the alternative is to have it at the front, here.' I pointed at a spot next to the front doors. 'The blast takes out the tables at the street end, everyone at the bar and most of the area alongside it. Then everyone at the back panics, and they all have to climb over the wounded to get out. More damage, more chaos, more of a statement. All it needs is a ten-second timer from when it's planted, which means that there's no window for a do-gooder to get in there and try to give it back. All the trigger man has to do is make sure he's behind the blast cone.'

'Nice thinking. We're loading it with about five kilos of bolts, too, so that should work nicely.' Graeme was obviously pleased with himself, and with my contribution. I leant over the plans to check a couple of details and noticed a spot where the name of the pub had been written in pencil and rubbed out. The something Swan, by the look of it, which meant I now had an awful lot more to work with than before.

'When's it going ahead?'

'Saturday. You'll be looking after the bag until then. We'll come to you, arm the device and deliver it to the lucky boy. All you need to do is keep your mouth shut – you won't have a problem with that, will you?'

'No.'

'Good.'

Half an hour later we were on our way back to my place, with a home-made anti-personnel mine on the seat behind me.

At the flat, I put the bag up on the dining table and started to study it. Perfectly innocuous, just the sort of thing you see tourists carrying every day in the capital – which was the point. Nobody would look at this twice, and you'd need to be really paying attention to notice where the seams had been reinforced to hold the weight of explosives and carefully packed metal. There was a safety trip, too, designed to fire the device if the bag was opened for examination, but that hadn't been armed yet. I decided that this was my advantage, and if I had any chance at all of stopping this from going down it lay right in front of me.

Taking the device out of its bag was a delicate operation – I didn't want to risk leaving things in a condition that hinted at tampering. I slid the bag down around the bomb and put it to one side. The detonator's place was empty, a safety measure to stop it from going off in my flat, but also to prevent me from trying to get clever with it. It made perfect sense, and while it was a bit obvious, I could see someone desperate to prevent the job from going ahead choosing to tamper with that. Fortunately, I had something considerably sneakier in mind.

I scooped out a small section from one of the plastique blocks, from the side facing out towards the blast cone. Putting the spare explosive to one side, I grabbed a knife from the kitchen and sliced into my thumb. A thin red line appeared where the edge had passed, shortly followed by a large drop of my blood. That went into the hole I'd carved, as did several more, then I stuck my thumb under a tap while I grabbed a plaster. I heal pretty quickly, but there was no point making a mess. Rubber gloves on for the next bit, as I covered over my little marker and smoothed the surface until there was no sign I'd ever been there. The metalwork went carefully back into position, then I checked to see that everything was as I'd found it before sliding the whole thing back into its bag and dumping it in the wardrobe to await pickup.

Next was letting the folks back home know what was going on. We'd assumed that there was a danger of me being watched on the astral plane as well as the material, but I figured there was less risk attached for the former when it came to emergency contact and this seemed like a pretty good reason to take the chance. Not only that, the odds of me being watched on the material plane were now so high that I didn't dare try my standard contact procedure even though it had been displayed as normal behaviour for months now.

I took a long, hot shower, pausing to flush the tiny lump of explosive down the toilet on the way, and then stretched out naked on the bed to get my breathing right. A Lynyrd Skynyrd album covered the sound just enough to prevent anyone listening in from realising that I was sliding into a meditative trance rather than regular sleep, and then my perceptions started to shift and the world faded out around me.

I was standing on an empty plain: grey, bleak and not too dissimilar from the place where the dead usually hang out. Above me were the stars, clear and precise as though there was no atmosphere. The sound of my breath was muted, dull and almost hollow. I was in a place that both does and does not exist, a place between worlds where secrets are currency and how smart and strong you are is all that matters. I quite like it there, actually – it's refreshingly honest most of the time.

My destination was on the horizon: a tower that marked where the Service keeps its lookouts in that place. A quick mantra lifted my feet from the ground and then I was gliding towards it at a pace much faster than I could have managed on foot. Hey, why walk when you don't have to?

The tower was a copy of the Tower of London, specifically the White Tower at its heart – one of the oldest bastions of British defence. It was an appropriate metaphor – I don't know how long the Service has been doing this kind of thing, but magicians have been guarding our shores from attack for thousands of years. I might not look much like an old Celtic shaman in the flesh, but the job I do really isn't all that different from what they did back then. I'm just a little bit sneakier.

The guardians at the gate were twice my size and didn't look overly chuffed to see me. I watched them observing me as I approached, their huge heads lowering as my range decreased, and eventually I landed at their feet.

'What manner of creature is this?' a voice boomed, apparently from the gate itself. 'Speak name and purpose, creature, lest you pay the price of trespass.'

I do wish they'd update the thing.

'I am but a traveller in the cold wastes,' I replied, 'hungry and in need of shelter from those who wish to harm me. I seek the succour of my friends, who are inside this place, and would share counsel with them.' It's a bloody awful speech, but they tell me there are good reasons for it. One of these days someone might even tell me what those reasons are.

'Enter, traveller. Take warmth by our fire, and rest in our hall. You are welcome.' The doors swung open and I walked inside.

There wasn't a lot to do while I waited. It's not like a proper waiting room with out-of-date magazines or a tankful of fish to stare vacantly at. All I could do was cool my heels while someone who was authorised to hear my report was found and gated in. Without any reference points, there was no way of telling how long I waited, either, although time in places like this doesn't exactly relate to what's happening in the 'real' world very well to start with. So I stood in the bare stone room, humming a dirty song about penguins that my unarmed-combat instructor had brought back from his time in the Falklands.

Eventually a door opened, and in walked the Boss himself. Obviously someone had decided I was worth getting him here in person, and judging by the look on his face I was rather glad not to be that poor unfortunate someone. If the old man wasn't happy with my report, that someone would probably be guarding a stone circle somewhere really unpleasant by the end of the week. I stood up straight and nodded to him. 'Sir.'

'What's this about, then? You'd better have something good to use this method of contact.' As ever, he was all smiles and hearty welcome.

'My group are planning to bomb a pub, probably in the West End of London, on Saturday.'

'Are they, now? Is this a good time to wrap them up, then?'

'No, sir, I don't think it is. I'm finally making a little progress and seeing what's behind the group I've joined. We need to prevent the plan from going ahead in such a way that I'm not exposed.'

'Are you sure about stopping it?'

'Yes, sir, I am. There's no profit for me in this, and the last thing we need is another bomb going off in London right now. In fact, if we play it cleverly enough, this might just get me in a little further.'

'Right. What do you suggest?'

'The bomb's marked with my blood, inside the explosive component, so it should be easy enough for a remote viewer to track, and they're using home-cooked plastic so there should be plenty for dogs to go on. I'd suggest intercepting the carrier on his way to the target and giving the impression that the authorities are trying to make a tip-off look like a random sweep. I've also got a patsy in mind, so if you can set him up from your end, that'll keep my nose clean.'

'OK, I'll approve that. Be aware that you'll get some attention from Special Branch or MI5, though. If they hold off, then your people will know there's something wrong. Try not to get arrested, will you?'

'Yes, sir. Although tracking the device to our patsy, then arresting him and letting him go might be useful.'

'I can't control the Met that closely. But I'll see what I can do.'

'Thank you, sir.'

'Now tell me who you've marked out as the patsy and go home. I've got work to do.'

'Certainly, sir. I think the best patsy for this would be Graeme Flory.'

Chapter Six

I'd quite fancied putting Michael up as the patsy, but since I didn't have any evidence that he was involved, that was something of a non-starter. Graeme, on the other hand, was in it right up to his skinny neck – and I owed him for sucker-punching me on my first night at the club. Besides, I was becoming more and more convinced that Martin was really in charge and Graeme was an obstacle to my getting closer to him. Either way, I was now in a pretty substantial position of trust and Graeme's removal would open a vacancy that I might be able to exploit. It was a good place to be: there was some action going on at last and I was right in the middle of it.

Tuesday's morning run had some unexpected company when Graeme joined me half a mile in. While I officially had no idea where he lived, and thus no reason to doubt that he lived nearby, it was a pretty good bet that he'd have had to make a special trip to intercept me. His appearance wasn't exactly a surprise: he'd undoubtedly want to keep an eye on the guy holding the baby, and this was an effective way to hint to me that I'd better be a good boy if I wanted to see the weekend. His conversation was minimal, thankfully, and we concentrated on keeping up a brisk pace, with both of us occasionally pushing the other. It was a good run, and I got home a few minutes earlier than I normally would have to see an unmarked white van pulling out of my building's car park. Something about that made me suspicious in the extreme, although Graeme didn't bat an eyelid and was quite happy to come in for an orange juice. I left him alone in the front room while I got ready for work, since if that van hadn't been somebody trying to wire my place up I might as well let Graeme do it instead. After all, I had nothing to hide ...

Graeme was with me the next morning, too, and of course there was the club that night. I was told in no uncertain terms to get an early night, since they didn't want me getting into any trouble between then and the weekend.

Thursday passed, too. Drinks with Michael in the evening, and food at a nice little Indian restaurant where he was an embarrassing asshole. I made sure not to eat any of his dishes, to be on the safe side. Just as I was starting to think of him as a pitiable figure, he had to step up and remind me exactly how objectionable he was. What amused me was how much he was like Gary and his mates. If he hadn't worked so hard to shed the accent and gain the money, he'd have fitted right in. Served him right, really.

Friday was distraction activity. I picked up a woman in a bar, went back to her place and vented a pretty significant amount of frustration, then pleaded work that needed doing and left her just before dawn. This asshole thing was becoming second nature.

And so Saturday arrived with me smelling of expensive perfume and feeling an awful lot better about the world, even if the woman I'd just left would have felt better if I hadn't had to go. I went back to the flat, had a shower, found some clean clothes and waited for someone to come and pick the bag up.

And waited.

And waited.

'Hurry up and wait' is all very well, and the flat was an awful lot more comfortable than some of the places I've done it, but there's only so much television I can stand to watch and I really wasn't in the mood to read. I paced a little, did some t'ai chi and generally killed time until the doorbell finally rang at half-past five in the evening. Of course, with my luck they'd have shown up early if I'd stuck around with my new friend.

It was Graeme again, with a serious face. I let him in, pulled the bag out of its hiding place in the wardrobe and handed it over with an appearance of relief.

'Good luck, mate.' It seemed like the right thing to say.

'Cheers, John. Get your coat.'

'I thought—'

'Just to the rendezvous. Once it's handed over, you're in the clear.'

Another drive with the bag behind me. Mr White was waiting for us in a lay-by, and checked over the device to make sure I hadn't messed around with it. I must have put the thing back together properly, since he seemed happy enough to fit the detonator, arm the tamper switch and step back.

'Thank you, gentlemen,' he said. 'Best of British.' And with that he was gone, slipping into the shadows.

We drove on some more, until another empty lay-by came up. Graeme told me to put the bag behind a sign warning that dumping would be prosecuted, and after that we went to the pub. Martin was already there, and we had a quiet evening waiting to hear the news roll in about how our little project had gone. As methods of keeping someone on ice went, it was better than holding me at gunpoint in a disused warehouse, and I managed to get them talking about their time in the Army. Nothing relevant came out, but it was all good background.

We'd dropped off the bag at seven o'clock in the evening. Putting things together after the event, this was the story I managed to reconstruct:

At ten minutes past seven, a white van pulled into the lay-by to allow the driver to nip into the bushes to relieve himself.

When he emerged he was carrying the bag. He got into the van, pulled out into traffic and headed towards the centre of London.

Just after half-past seven, he found traffic snarled up by an accident that had closed the road. Emergency vehicles were on the scene and clearing things away, and nobody was actually hurt. This kept him stuck for about half an hour.

At eight o'clock, he managed to get off the main road and into suburbia. A succession of roadworks managed to get him quite thoroughly lost and he ended up coming into town by an entirely unplanned route. He was already looking edgy by this point, since when he'd been instructed in the manner of firing the device he'd also been warned to get it into position sooner rather than later. The look on his face when he was caught by a traffic camera was not that of a happy man.

Eight-fifteen found him looking at the queue for a random vehicle inspection being run by the Metropolitan Police. He decided that he'd rather not join in, and turned off the road into a conveniently placed yard. Just as he was supposed to. Presumably he was planning to get on the Tube and make his way to the target that way, but the presence of the Met's Anti-Terrorist Squad, complete with a large number of armed officers in body armour just itching to get the tear gas out, must have made him change his mind. I know it would have changed mine.

A challenge was issued, and the carrier seemed to at least think about it. He kept his hands on the wheel as he'd been told for a good couple of minutes as officers approached the vehicle. He was fully covered, carefully watched and on the verge of being arrested when he reached down beside him. Three officers opened fire, hitting him twice in the shoulder – presumably they thought he was going for a gun. He wasn't.

The explosion started in the van's front, as you'd expect, then tore backwards through the vehicle, which absorbed most of the shrapnel that was meant for the pub's occupants. The carrier was goo in less than a tenth of a second, but some of those projectiles kept on going. Less than a second after those three shots were fired, five police officers were on their backs: two had lumps of metal in their body armour, one was missing an arm, one was probably going to limp for the rest of his life and the last one no longer had much in the way of a head. There were other minor injuries, some hearing damage and a lot of shattered nerves, but one dead policeman was far less than the thing had been meant to produce. That didn't make me feel any better about seeing one of the good guys go down, though.

Back in the pub, we all reacted badly when the news came through. My reasons were a little different from Graeme and Martin's, of course, but I didn't have to act disappointed when I was genuinely pissed off at the presence of casualties. I would have expected there to be a sniper handy to take the carrier out, but apparently the angles weren't right or something. Nevertheless, the plan had been shitcanned and we were already speculating as to how the authorities found out about it.

Graeme was straight on to me as a possible leak, but Martin pointed out that I hadn't known the target or the time that the attack was due to go ahead – as evidenced by me sitting in my flat all day waiting. I'd been with them from the moment I knew the plan was under way, so there was no chance of me having slipped off to call anyone either.

What really bothered them was the way that the vehicle had been deflected from its planned route and pushed into a location that it shouldn't have been anywhere near. When I pointed out that whoever had called this in must have known the carrier's part of the plan, both parties went very quiet indeed. I wondered how many people knew that part of the plan, and just how many of them were no longer thought as absolutely trustworthy as they had been half an hour earlier. Nothing wrong with sowing a little doubt and discord among the enemy, and this would force them to look at the whole affair very seriously indeed.

My run the next morning was unaccompanied, which was just as well. The markers were in place for me to expect a message. The communications van was in its appointed place and as I passed it the voice filled my ears with digital sweetness:

'The Met managed to intercept the bomb with minimal casualties, none of which were civilian. Unfortunately, the carrier, who has not yet been identified, killed himself by detonating the bomb early rather than be captured. We've deposited a thousand pounds in Flory's bank account and generated a tip-off in his voice, which is now on record at New Scotland Yard. Your report on Mr White has yielded a number of possible suspects, so try to get more information on him if you can. Be aware that this matter is now the subject of a police investigation and MI5 are also likely to take an interest, so keep as low a profile as possible. Message ends.'

Nothing I didn't already know, really, although the news had said that the bomb went off accidentally at a routine checkpoint. Mr White had obviously intended to be an enigma, so I'd just have to hope that I ran into him again, and in the meantime keep an eye out for any new faces in the neighbourhood in case it was MI5 trying to poke about a bit. I didn't want the boys from Thames House to get in my way and risk honking up the bigger game for the sake of a few losers in an East End gym, so if they showed up I'd have to hope that we could pull them back a bit before they messed up my pitch.

Back at the office on Monday, Michael seemed to have no idea about the weekend's entertainment beyond what had been on the news. In fact, he appeared to be out of the loop generally, which made me wonder why he was so desperate to be part of it. Perhaps it was wanting to belong somewhere, a common enough feeling in modern society and one that groups like this use to pull people in. His allusion to another group had never been followed up, however, and I figured it was time to push him on it over a drink.

'Oh, they're much more upscale, and I'm in the doghouse a bit for hanging out at the gym because they think it's beneath me. A good bunch, though, and I'll see if I can introduce you to one or two of them, just to see if you get along. They're very picky about who gets in, of course – can't have people blabbing about who's who and what's what, eh?' Frankly, it sounded like bullshit, like he was trying to puff himself up a bit in response to how well I'd slotted in at the club. That didn't stop him from going on a bit more, though. 'Much more interesting people, too. The sort of people who might do your career a bit of a favour, if you catch my drift.' I knew that Michael had some big-money clients, and maybe these were the people he was talking about. Certainly the funding had to come from some-where, so perhaps Michael was making himself useful by generating it.

Michael made a point of grabbing me at the club that Wed-nesday just as I was on my way to join Gary and the lads. 'Don't,' he said. 'Not if you want to get along. Mixing with that sort might get you into more trouble than you'd like. I heard a rumour that they've become enough of a nuisance to actually get something done about it.' I sent Gary on his way and went back west with Michael instead. 'To be honest, John, I'm probably not going again after tonight. You might want to consider doing the same.'

The warning, and its timing, caught my curiosity. If Michael was bullshitting, he might just have been trying to get me back into his pocket, a position from which I'd obviously slipped some time ago. If he wasn't, it hinted at connections beyond those I'd already seen, and placed him much closer to the centre of things than I'd previously thought. I hadn't learned much about him from Gary and company, and Graeme and Martin had other things to talk about, so from that angle Michael was a bit of a mystery. I promised to consider his advice as we parted company, and started to think that progress was coming from an unexpected direction.

Chapter Seven

Another week of being a good boy, making money and acting like an arse. The cover had become second nature a while back, and to be honest I was pretty much doing everything but the actual trading in my sleep. There was a kind of excitement to that, at least, but it was far more intense for the people around me who had a genuine interest in it. I couldn't complain about the money, though, since I was pulling in an absolute packet in commission and bonuses off the back of my successes both real and engineered. The latter had been calmed down a bit during the previous month or two, since I had less to prove once my feet were firmly under the desk, and it was better to stay in the pack a bit more and allow most of the people I was working with to forget me in the background. It would make my eventual departure easier, too, since office people seem to be very good at forgetting their colleagues once they're out of sight for a bit. The last thing I need is someone recognising me from a previous job and trying to engage me in conversation by the wrong name.

When the next Wednesday came around, I decided to take Michael's advice and give the club a miss. We went to a tiny little restaurant off New Oxford Street and ate incredible veal cutlets washed down with a wine whose price tag would have kept me in food for a month. This was a part of the job I was definitely getting into – nice clothes, gourmet food and fine wines may not seem like much from the outside but once you get into the habit they're a rewarding hobby. The chocolate soufflé was divine, washed down with a sweet dessert wine and capped by brandy that cost almost as much per glass as the wine had per bottle. Compared to a night of brutality, cheap lager and laddish crap, this was heaven. I had to remind myself that it was work, and that the man sitting opposite me was part of my assignment. Fortunately, it transpired that I was part of his that evening.

'I've been talking to some people, John, and we think it might be time for you to be introduced to one or two more of us. You might have been fitting in down at the gym, but it's obvious that you're better than that and we think you might have potential for a more interesting role in society.'

'Society?' It was an interesting choice of word, and the way he said it gave me the impression that he wasn't necessarily talking about society in general.

'You know what I mean. Why hang around with louts when you might have a chance to make an actual difference? Decisions aren't made on the streets, John, they're made in quiet rooms with nice addresses. Perhaps you might just have what it takes to help shape those decisions.'

This was what I'd been waiting for: a door to the next level. It made all the crap I'd put up with back in the East End suddenly worth something – an investment coming to the point of maturity. I made interested noises, and Michael told me that Gary and his lads were starting to become the focus of police attention as a result of their hunting expeditions. I was glad to hear it, since those nights when we went looking for victims were really taking it out of me. It's not as if I'm averse to violence as a method of getting what I want, but I prefer my violence to have a *purpose*. I don't use it indiscriminately, and prefer other options when they're available. The idea of having to put the boot into someone for no reason other than the colour of their skin came close to making me sick. I assured Michael that I'd be staying out of the club's way for a while to give justice time to be served, which made him happy enough to get another round of brandies in.

Wednesday night seemed to be Nazi night, given that the meeting Michael had talked about happened a week after that dinner. We were in a private dining room deep in the City, and Michael had been joined by an older man who was introduced as Mr Gold. This fellow was obviously another money man, but on a level way above myself and Michael – Mr Gold looked like the type who plans economies rather than deals, the sort of money that shapes market trends and has Cabinet ministers over for tea. I had quite definitely moved up a level. The restaurant was the kind that did basic food really well, lots of roasted meat, a small range of vegetables and sticky desserts to finish. In fairness, the food was pretty damn good, since they were only interested in the best ingredients. The menu didn't even mention prices, which was a hint that the place wasn't exactly cheap.

The pseudonyms, on the other hand, were obvious enough to be laughable. While they might have had some kind of reasoning to which I wasn't privy, from my point of view it was starting to look like a bad Tarantino knock-off. Part of me was waiting for someone to start talking about 70s soul records for no readily apparent reason.

Luckily for me, though, Mr Gold wasn't interested in talking about James Brown. After casting his beady eye over me, he started asking me about my background – family, school, my time in the Army and a whole pile of seemingly random stuff including food and drink. What caught my attention was the tingle down my spine as he was asking the questions, as though he were using some kind of magic on me either to compel answers or check their truthfulness. Either way I was safe, since I was happy to answer anything he wanted to ask and had drilled my cover to the point where it felt more like real life than my real life.

After a good hour of this, and a soup starter, we turned to more esoteric subjects. Michael's observation that I had occult books at home led to a number of questions along that line. Mr Gold seemed pretty well informed himself, and had no problem discussing Levi, Crowley, Mathers and Agrippa in some detail, pushing me on my experiences, opinions and practices, along with checking for any affiliations I might have had in that direction. I admitted that I'd thought about a couple of groups, but not liked the idea of how they operated. Mr Gold sympathised, and carefully said nothing regarding his own position.

By the time we got to dessert we were onto politics. I was playing the calm and reasonable card here and fitting in nicely – a major contrast to the rabid hate I had to play along with when I was out with Gary. Here again I got to do most of the talking while questions guided and cross-referenced my responses. But as interrogations go, this was by far the nicest I'd ever experienced. I doubted that if they were to come at me as anything other than a friend the treatment would be anywhere near as civilised. We spoke of immigration controls, and deportation, and how socialism had shackled the independence of business. We agreed that something had to be done to get the situation back onto the rails, and that manipulating the government wasn't having anywhere near enough effect to make a difference. The new anti-terror laws were a good thing, though, since they enabled the population to be controlled more efficiently and in such a way that they were grateful for it.

The atmosphere in that room was definitely one that had little respect for the common man. I've heard many types of people expound a similar attitude over the years, calling them cattle, sheeple or any one of a host of references to dumb animals that need to be controlled. Normally it's rooted in the need to feel superior while being stuck on the outside, a reaction to being outside the norm either by choice or circumstance. Here it was different: this was talk from very much inside the Establishment, where people of power could put their views into practice by influencing politicians, and just plain buying them when necessary.

Mr Gold was happy to sign for dinner, so I must have done something right. He shook my hand, told me that it had been a pleasure and commended Michael on his choice of friends. Michael was quite obviously delighted, although he waited until we were alone before he showed it. Then it was all smiles and 'well done' and a quick drink in a nearby pub before it was time to get our heads down.

It was nice to have something to report, too. I jumped through all the hoops of sending Mr Gold's details back to the Boss, in the vague hope that he might be identified more readily than Mr White. Perhaps once I got in I'd be able to start pinning down a few real names ready to be rolled up – I certainly hoped so.

The morning also brought interesting news: Gary and his lads had been arrested in connection with a number of the beatings they'd been handing out. It seemed that they'd been spotted last time, and the pub identified to the police, who were only too happy to pick them up as they arrived for their drinks between practice and application. There was no mention of Graeme or Martin, and I hoped that there wouldn't be. If the trace went back to the club it could come back to Michael and myself. Michael seemed far less concerned than I was when I mentioned it to him.

'Relax, John. Why do you think I suggested you get out when I did? The plod have got their men, and there won't be any need to take it further. Just keep your nose clean in future, right?'

'So the fix is in, then?'

'Oh yeah. Some people take orders, some give them. We're in the second category.'

So the gang had been hung out to dry, then. Obviously they'd become too much of a liability, and now Graeme would have to find a new bunch of stormtroopers to beat up. Much as I wished otherwise, I was sure he wouldn't have too much trouble finding one.

Being invited out for a pint with Martin was something of a surprise, but he was just trying to make sure that I was keeping my mouth shut. He had the good manners not to threaten me openly, but made it very clear that I was in it right up to my neck now and anything I said would take me down just as firmly as the rest of them. He also suggested that my stay in prison would be short, but not because of an early release. 'Prison's dangerous, John, and they really don't like people who tell tales, if you see my point.'

This was really good news again. Threatening me in such a subtle fashion indicated that they might want to use me again, but any enquiries I made in that direction were deflected. 'Not my decision, mate. I leave that sort of thing to the men in charge.' Martin wasn't about to tell me who they were, but it made sense that Mr White was one of them, and by the same token Mr Gold seemed likely to have a part in it. Where this left Michael, I wasn't sure. He seemed to bridge both camps, but apparently as an acolyte to each. His attachment to the more important group made the tolerance he was shown at the club more understandable, as did his withdrawal from it when things started to look dodgy. There must have been a sympathiser inside the local police, too, to provide that warning and keep the investigation from spreading out to include Graeme, Martin, Michael and myself. A network was starting to become apparent within which I could move forward.

But there was even better news to come. Martin had one more

warning for me before the end of the night. 'We'll call you, all right? Keep quiet for now, and stay away from Graeme completely for a bit. He's starting to get the wrong kind of attention.' If I was right, then that was the beginning of his downfall as the information planted by the Service started to become apparent to his controllers. It couldn't happen to a nicer bloke.

Michael and I spent more time together, talking politics more frequently now that we knew we were sympathetic to one another. There was much talk of how the Prime Minister's agenda didn't match ours, and how something really should be done about it once he'd finished putting in the mechanisms of control that were required for a more efficient state. The fear being built up in the populace was a good thing because it made bringing those measures to bear all the easier, and it wouldn't be long before the people were crying out for more – for identity cards, DNA registration and curbs to the right of free assembly. With those in place, the elimination of undesirable elements could begin – through repatriation, mainly, but also with imprisonment for those we couldn't send away. The unions could be destroyed by a few well-placed scandals taking effective leaders out of play and replacing them with loyal citizens who knew how to toe the party line. With those measures implemented, manufacturing could be revitalised, an industrial base rebuilt and Britain's place in the world elevated to the glory days of Empire. Conscription would return, too, as a means of indoctrinating the young before they entered the workforce. It would take a while, maybe fifty years or so, but the results would be magnificent. A new Golden Age was coming, and with support from America, where similar plans were apparently under way, a new North Atlantic Treaty would see two strong nations standing side by side to secure peace throughout the world.

This was not a plan I much liked the sound of. Some of those mechanisms helped me do my job, certainly, and the way that databases were integrating made it a lot easier to find people of interest to me and the Service. But the rest of it wouldn't work; someone would start shouting the right things, a movement would begin and no matter how many you locked up or shot, there'd still be more. I don't have much faith in people – it's a side effect of the job – but I have faith in that. I was going to make sure that the plan didn't happen, though, because while the system might need bastards like me as servants it really doesn't need to have them as leaders.

More time passed at the bank, including my six-month appraisal. Everyone was very happy, apparently, and I was considered an asset to the trading floor (although the joke about getting me insured and put in the inventory for later sell-off fell completely flat). There was a pay rise from merely overpaid to grossly overpaid, a pile of bonuses that made me think about buying a holiday home, and a bottle of champagne that seemed to be thrown in just for the hell of it. The targets might have been shits, but I had to admit that the cover had a certain something going for it.

Another thing I somehow managed to do was get a thing going with the woman I'd had to abandon on the day of the bombing, which provided much-needed stress relief, a bit of exercise in the shape of trips to the gym and a reason not to screw any of the girls at work. The options there were attractive, but I firmly believe that sleeping with colleagues is a bad idea, especially when undercover. A nicely running operation can be bollocksed up by an angry girlfriend screaming her head off in public, especially in the place where you're supposed to work, and it's a risk I've managed to avoid taking so far. Sarah, the woman in question, wasn't looking for anything serious either, so we spent time together, ate food, drank wine and shagged like bunnies when the opportunity arose. It was my idea of a perfect relationship, to be honest: no embarrassing confessions, no need for messing around with excessive intimacy and no strings attached. I was going to have to think about dating a City girl again if they were all like this.

I was still spending time with Michael, of course – Sarah wasn't going to get in the way of the main job at hand, or 'more important matters', as I put it to him. He thought I was wasting my time with her when there were plenty of other girls whose eye I'd apparently caught, but there was a tactic in play here – being sufficiently similar to him was enough. If I moulded my personality too closely to his it might have looked suspicious, and this way I was close enough to Michael to keep him happy while staying inside the profile that I thought the group wanted to see – stable, but not overly tied down. It was a balancing act, but I was pretty sure I'd got it right.

Chapter Eight

Another month passed before I was invited to have dinner with Mr Gold again, and this time he brought a friend. Mr Green was another patrician type – in late middle age and obviously well-used to the authority he carried with him. Another round of questions, but this time we focused more on esoteric matters before moving on to a rehash of the ideas I'd previously discussed with Michael. Mr Green's language, however, was not that of the businessman. Here we had a definite civil servant.

I had to be getting somewhere for a second grown-up to be willing to meet me, and while we talked about magic and its applications I could see that I'd pitched myself about right. They were just impressed enough, not so much that it would worry them, but they had the impression of someone who'd been studying the subject for a while and knew what he was talking about. More than Michael did, that's for sure – we left him behind in about half an hour and he spent the rest of the conversation looking like a schoolboy who'd walked into a class on advanced quantum theory. We talked about god-forms, their summoning and control, how one identified the means of invocation and evocation, protective measures and what one did before and after the operation. All good, solid stuff, and they were coming from a very traditional background – lots of old rituals, with a touch of North European on the side. This last detail tied in nicely with the papers from Camden, and provided a sure sign of being on the right track.

It was suggested that I might be the sort of person their group would like to have as a member, and I suggested that I might be interested in such a thing since I was currently working alone and would value the experience that came with other, more practised magicians. Watching Michael was a revelation here, since it was clear that such an invitation hadn't been extended to him. Moreover, he had the look of a man who thought he deserved such an invitation far more than I did, which meant he was either a bigger idiot than I thought, acting fit to win a slew of awards, or possessed of information he wasn't sharing. It didn't matter much – I was getting closer to my objective and he was therefore becoming irrelevant at long last. Deep-cover work doesn't allow you to use the kind of discretion that's normally applied in choosing friends, since it's about how useful a person is rather than whether or not you actually like them, so having a reason to lose Michael's company was a good thing as far as I was concerned. After all these months of making him my bosom buddy, if he dropped me in a fit of pique I'd not only have the relief of his absence but a lack of messy fallout from trying to get rid of him in a way that didn't attract suspicion.

So I went away happy, and got back to the waiting game. More work, a little bit of social life and a lot of impatience to finally get the game started. After seven months working in the bank I was beginning to go stir-crazy, and was itching for a good old-fashioned stand-up fight against the Forces of Darkness. It's the waiting that kills me every time, having to let the enemy trust me enough to allow me inside their guard so that when the strike comes it can do as much damage as possible. There are other methods that can get you enough information to take a group out of circulation, but cleaning up after them can be troublesome and you won't always get a complete picture of what's been going on – which is very useful if you want to remove or mitigate the effects of a group's actions as well. That means you have to wait, and wait, and wait – until the moment finally comes when one swift sequence of actions can take the whole apparatus out before it has time to react against you. The theory is simple, even if the practice can be tedious in the extreme.

Of course, the involvement of a high-ranking civil servant didn't help matters here either, and demonstrated why the Service is so insulated from everyone else. If I were working for MI5, and Mr Green was a senior member of that department or its oversight structure, the job would be dead in the water, as would I some short time afterwards. The indications that this group had someone inside the police who could influence an investigation were another reason to be glad that we kept our operations secret from other authorities, as a request for support could have turned into another point of failure.

It doesn't half get lonely sometimes.

Michael and I stayed friendly, although a little distance was creeping in over the next week. Then his irritation seemed to cool and he brought me back into his close circle again for reasons I didn't get and he wasn't willing to explain. I simply acted glad that the invitation to join the group hadn't got in the way of our friendship. 'Oh, I shouldn't worry about that, John,' he said. 'I think this will make us closer than ever.' Great.

I was relaxing at home one evening a couple of weeks later when a knock sounded at the door, the kind of knock that said, 'If you don't open this door pretty quickly, I'm coming straight through it.' Deciding that aggressive remodelling wouldn't do the flat any favours, I caught a quick look through the camera and saw someone who looked like he wouldn't have much of a problem walking through the door. Big enough, probably around six feet or so, and wide enough to make it look almost short. I opened the door to examine the behemoth in detail.

He was about an inch shorter than me, which would make him six feet tall, and had shoulders that made me look like a fashion model. Short dark hair was cropped close to his skull and the brown eyes that examined me had a hint of coldness that spoke volumes about his likely competence in a fight. The build was solid, almost compact in spite of its obvious bulk, and gave an impression of some serious strength.

'Mr Dennis?' His voice was deep, sure, but not the rumble you might expect. The Northern accent was a small surprise after all these London lads, and held a note of education to it. We were out of thug territory and into a completely different level of bastard – one that had a right to think of itself as professional.

'Yes?' There wasn't much else to say, really.

'My name is Folkestone. Mr Green and Mr Gold send their compliments and would like you to join them.' It wasn't a request, but at least the guy made it sound reasonably polite.

'Now?'

'Now.'

'Right. I'll get my coat, then.'

'That won't be necessary.'

'Oh.'

We took the stairs down into the basement garage where a van was waiting for us with the engine running. Folkestone put me in the back, where I couldn't help noticing the lack of windows, and slid the door shut on me. I'd spotted a seat in there, so I loaded myself into it while the van shifted from Folkestone's weight getting comfortable in the front. I found a seatbelt and snapped it shut just as we were pulling out. I've been thrown around in the back of vans once or twice before, so it was nice to take a ride in some comfort for a change. We drove around for a while, but judging by some of the turns we took there were quite a few switchbacks and false moves made to disorientate me, so I wouldn't be able to pinpoint my destination.

A good sign, that, since if they were just going to kill me I doubted that they'd take the trouble to get me lost first. In time, we came to a stop at the bottom of a ramp. The door opened and Folkestone was there, offering me a largeish black bag. 'Put this on, please.' I slipped the bag over my head and was led away from the van, to whatever fate these people had planned for me.

Having a bag over your head is a strange experience the first few times it happens, but I got used to it when I was being selected for my job in the Service. I lost count of the number of times I was transported from place to place without being allowed to know points A and B – or anywhere in between them – and while it's a bit disorientating at first, you can acclimatise to the loss of visual input and the stuffy sensation you get from being trapped with your own stale breath. One top tip for that is to avoid stinky cheese if you think a bag over your head is a serious possibility, and likewise anything with too much garlic. You might not smell your breath out in the fresh air, but when it's accreting in front of your nose things can get a bit too flavour-filled for comfort. In fact, it's one of the moments that make carrying a packet of breath mints such a good idea – just remember to ask *nicely* before they put the bag on, and hope that the other party doesn't think it's a cyanide pill or something equally silly.

Folkestone led me along a corridor, one without windows by the sounds our footsteps made, and through a set of doors to a point where he left me. I opened my ears, trying to pick out sounds, and used my 'other' sense to try to find anything near me. The place had power, that was certain, and felt like it might be a temple of some kind. There was a gentle buzzing down the back of my spine, and I was starting to feel just a tiny bit light-headed. My guess was that some kind of ritual was either about to happen or was going on very close by. Perhaps I had finally arrived in the belly of the beast . . .

Suddenly, the hood was torn off from behind me and a set of lights came on that were too bright for the hood to have blocked out. I was standing in the middle of a circular room about twenty feet in diameter and ten feet high beneath a vaulted ceiling. I couldn't get much more detail than that thanks to the lights all around, and the four robed figures in front of me. Another such figure joined the group from behind me as I tried to take the situation in, presumably the person who'd removed my own hood. Each was dressed in black, with a mask to hide their faces from me, and the robes were cut loose enough to prevent me from getting any real detail of their physiques. I could tell, however, that Folkestone wasn't one of them – he was physically distinctive, and the marquee he'd need to hide that figure would have made a kaftan look like a catsuit. These were average-looking, probably male judging by height, and the one who'd taken my hood didn't walk like a female. In fact, the one who'd taken my hood walked more like a soldier than anything else – I was thinking Mr White for that one. A brief moment of consideration matched his height, too. Experiences like this are supposed to awe the person under scrutiny, but I wasn't wasting the time they gave me. I let them see a suitable expression, but my mind was racing.

The five were spread around me in a semicircle, each about five feet apart and the same distance from me. There was no way I'd be able to take more than a couple before the others were able to get at me, and I had no idea what they might be carrying under those robes. If any of them was armed I'd have been in real trouble if I tried anything, and I was quite sure that Folkestone was within easy calling distance, no doubt with a couple of friends.

There was power in the room, too. I could feel it far more clearly now, since it seemed to be growing. The figures appeared to have grown a little, as well – I put that down to an energy effect, since it's easy enough to master as tricks go. I use the same trick occasionally, when I want to put a little more pressure on people; it kicks in all sorts of dominance and submission issues that sit in the back of the brain mostly minding their own business. I tried to look a bit impressed, but not too much.

'John Dennis.' Whoever was speaking had a microphone, since the voice was coming from every direction at once. 'It has been said that you wish to enter our company. Thus have you been brought before us.'

'What gives you the right to stand here?' Another voice, lighter than the first.

'What place do you think we have for you?' That was Mr White, I'd put money on it.

'Who are you to think that you deserve a place among us?' Hello, Mr Green.

'Why should we permit your entry to this place? The penalty for trespassing is death.' And hello, Mr Gold.

This was shaping up to be a fine old initiation in the traditional fashion. Of course, most of the time you get to find out what your lines as the aspirant are before you go in there, since the whole thing is a psychodrama designed to re-enact a metaphorical journey from darkness outside the group to the light inside it. I supposed that I'd just have to wing it and hope that I got through alive. Most groups don't actually kill you, despite all the dire threats, but in this case I wasn't so sure.

'I was called to this place, and thus I have come. It is not my place to ask why, nor to judge my worthiness. I seek only to learn, and hope that I might learn here. If death is the price of my search, I face it without fear.' Right, that covered everything they'd asked and shown the courage in the face of death that was traditional at times like this. It also sounded corny enough to be adequate for ritual purposes, since pretty much every ritual I've seen has a strong element of overacting and bad dialogue. Hey, it's not my idea – some people seem to actively enjoy this shit.

'Then we shall allow you to face a trial, that you may prove your worthiness to stand in our company. A place might be opened for you, but only at the expense of another. Would you take another's place in your search for knowledge?' It was the first voice again, one I didn't recognise but presumably the leader of the group. This was an interesting point – should I be willing to crawl over someone else to get in? Were they looking for ambition or a team player? Was this about enlightening the world or achieving power over it? I could make a case for each answer with the information I had to that point, so I was going to have to guess. Just when everything seemed to be going so well, too.

'I am.'

Silence.

The lights went out.

Bollocks.

When the lights came back on, only one robed figure remained. In front of him was a table holding a very sharp-looking knife and a packet of what looked like waxed paper, secured with ribbon and sealed with red wax. There was some kind of symbol on the seal that looked like a bird from my angle.

'We have met in conclave, and found the one whose place you may take. A brother who has broken our most sacred rule: the rule of silence. To silence him is the price of your admission to our ranks, and from this act you shall learn the cost of ill faith. Will you do this thing and stand among us?' He reached towards the knife, a gloved hand slipping out from under the robe. Lifting it, holding the point towards me, he continued, 'Or would you end it here, on the point of this knife? One way or another, it shall taste blood.'

'I will do as you ask, and take the place that shall be mine thereafter.' The man turned the knife so the hilt faced me, and

I took it. With the other hand, he lifted the packet and passed it across.

'Herein you shall find your quarry. Ensure he speaks no more.' The lights went out again for a few seconds. When they came back up I was alone; even the table had gone. That impressed me, since it was either much lighter than it looked or someone was a dab hand at shifting furniture.

There was nothing left to do at this point beyond opening my new orders. I couldn't fault these chaps for style, certainly, and the paper felt expensive under my fingers as I examined the packet. I'd guessed right about a bird on the seal: it was probably meant to be an eagle, its wings half-extended and head looking up and to the left. About time they gave me some kind of identifying mark to work with, even though I still didn't have a clue what they called themselves. Given that I don't even know the formal name of the Service I *really* work for, I couldn't exactly fault their tradecraft. I couldn't even identify any of their members yet, beyond descriptions of three people who were almost certainly powerful enough to defy suspicion if I was caught. Even with the Service behind me, I'd still be screwed if anything went wrong.

Time to break the seal and see what I was hunting. The wax came apart easily enough, and the ribbon fell away as I opened the folded outer paper to see what was inside. There was a single item – a photograph. Pictured was a face I'd come to know well . . .

Graeme Flory.

Chapter Nine

The trip back was just as mysterious, and I used the time to consider what I'd learned about my enemy. Assuming that this was the target group, I now had descriptions of four members – White, Green, Gold and Folkestone, an idea of their imagery from the seal and photo wrapping, and a person definitely involved with them somehow – Graeme Flory. Graeme was the question here: what to do about him? If it was a matter of killing him, then that was how it had to be, but I couldn't help wondering if there was some means of spiriting him away to become a useful intelligence source while convincing the target group of his demise. I'd have to give the impression of completely destroying his body, or of disposing of it in an unrecoverable fashion, and both are surprisingly difficult if you want a guaranteed result. Since I already knew that they were able to influence the police, any forensic evidence could be assumed available to them, and their access to Army records would also be a problem. Many things would need to be quietly fixed to arrange Graeme's disappearance, but I could at least suggest it.

When I got home, something was amiss, something I couldn't quite put my finger on. Checking around gave me the impression that someone else had been there, and that meant a search. A closer examination of the bookshelves gave it away: the dust had been disturbed across the whole thing, meaning someone had taken each book off the shelf and put it back again. That really wasn't a problem, since there was nothing to find. What might be a problem was that the place was now effectively bugged, and possibly even wired for cameras, given how small the damn things can be these days. Someone was going to get quite a show from Sarah's next visit if they'd wired the bedroom. Of course, I'd been assuming that the place was bugged from day one, so it wasn't going to make a great deal of difference to my routines except the one that involved contacting the Boss via dead-drop.

That left the astral plane as my only contact option, and even that was risky. I'd need to check a few things before I was willing to consider giving it a shot.

A magical ritual starts with a circle of protection, an established safe zone from which to work. This can be drawn with chalk, or salt, or certain formulations of mixed powder – or simply with clear focus and sheer force of will. This latter is my preferred method, since I don't like being tied to particular pieces of kit. It's a weakness in the field to be reliant on something you might not necessarily have with you, and any observer seeing two apparently different people with the same piece of kit might start putting two and two together to end up dead. It's not that I have any particular problem with necessary violence, just that I don't take any great pleasure in it and see no reason to suck people into that situation if I don't have to. Stupid people find enough ways to kill themselves anyway, and I'd much prefer the universe to weed out the dumb ones rather than me having to cull any more smart people – the smart/dumb ratio's bad enough as it is. So simple stuff like this is done without gear, and complicated bits of equipment are saved for complicated bits of sorcery.

Establishing a circle like this just takes practice, and once you've got the technique it's also the fastest way to get one done. That speed can save your life, and has saved mine more than once when unexpected nasties have popped out of nowhere. Once done, it's safe to extend the senses and take a look at what's happening beyond the physical – if you can see something that's only there in certain ways, then the odds are that it can see you. If it's hungry, aggressive or just plain evil, that can be a problem, and a good shield will stop most things like that from eating your head. There are some things that would walk straight through it, but happily those are rare and you generally need to do something really interesting to get their attention. Or be really mind-numbingly unlucky.

Senses opening out, seeing the astral superimposed on the physical world around me. Not crossing fully yet, just having a look for anything that shouldn't be there. They might easily have put some kind of guard dog on me to make sure I was behaving the way they expected me to, and I didn't want to show my hand while we were still in the early stages of the game. Shadows of otherness slipping across the edge of my peripheral vision, traces of people who'd been here before me, now long dead. Change the viewing angle, look past the dead, see what else is there. Some kind of track – something had been sniffing around but didn't appear to be there any more. Looking again in yet another way, and everything seemed to be clear. It was time to make a dash.

Across into the place where the Tower stood, through the guardians as quickly as I could and an urgent request for debrief. The Boss must have been better placed this time, since he was there in an effective jiffy.

'Sir, I need to get back ASAP. I've met the target group. They use the symbol of a bird. Green, White and Gold are identified by voice as members, but I've not seen their faces to confirm it. My inroad is to kill Flory for them, so we can guess that the set-up worked. I think we'd do better to bring him in if we can, but have no ideas for how to do that right now. Request instructions on that. Assume I'm being watched and that the dead-drop is blown. That is all.'

'Understood,' said the Boss. 'Go.'

I am on my way almost before the word is finished. Chasing through the gates, across the plain, moving as fast as I dare, for too much movement can attract certain attention. My kind walk in dangerous places, and we're not always the baddest bastards there. There's shit way worse than me in the universe.

The hairs on the back of my neck bristled as I heard what could have been a howl in the distance. A hunting dog? Some kind of predator? Difficult to say at long range, and not something I wanted to examine up close either way. The transition point was ahead, and with it the way back into my body and safety. The shadow I thought I saw as I passed back into the material was something I'd prefer to forget, but I foresaw a few nightmares over what had almost just been.

Whatever the Boss said, I was going to have to make preparations for Flory's death. Performance or truth, the steps would have to be taken for form's sake if nothing else, and a good clean kill benefits from preparation. I'd want chemicals for disposing of evidence, tools for the actual job and somewhere quiet to work. Since my instructions were to make sure he didn't tell anyone anything *ever again,* I assumed that this included the afterlife, which meant I'd need a few other bits and bobs to do the job properly. I hadn't been given a time frame, so I made sure to be thorough in my work rather than hurry and miss a trick or let a clue slip. First job was to find a lock-up that could be used as a base, and a little light disguise work allowed a dark-haired man with an ugly moustache to hire suitable premises for cash. Post 9/11 paranoia is one thing, but there's nothing like cash and a slightly bent landlord for getting around such inconveniences.

Next came arranging for certain powders to arrive at the lock-up, from different suppliers and using different names and a separate false address per order in case more than one used the same delivery company. I didn't want that particular combination being noticed before I'd had a chance to make use of them. Knives were simple, and the cookery training came in unexpectedly handy when picking the best tools for the job. Once again, I had to thank Chef for his patient instruction. Plastic sheeting, a predictable requirement, was easy and the protective suit so popular among forensic investigators came from a medical supply warehouse along with some surgical gloves and a suturing kit. Things would start coming together once people began tracking back from that address, but nothing I'd done up to that point would show up as unusual -- which was exactly what I wanted. If Graeme had to die, I wanted to be very sure indeed that he wasn't going to do me any damage from beyond the grave. I wasn't prepared to use magical ingredients from the standard suppliers, either. If I was going to keep this quiet I'd need to mix, brew and prepare everything myself from scratch. I did at least have the sense to use a cheap supermarket saucepan -- the good stuff I cooked food in would have been ruined, and that would never have done.

It was two weeks before things were ready, and I still hadn't heard from the Boss. Suboptimal, to say the least. Just to top it off, my morning run was provided with extra joy by Folkestone, who stood opposite the entrance of my building and tapped his watch when I noticed him. It seemed that people were becoming impatient with me.

The word finally came during the next morning's run. It was not a happy word, either. 'No options exist for retrieving Flory in a way that would guarantee operational success. Proceed as ordered by the target group. Message ends.' It was a hell of a way to kill a man, with two sentences from an electronic voice, but I was stuck without a choice. If I wanted to get into the group I'd have to do as I was told. I imagined that the Boss had thought about it for two minutes, sent an assistant to look at the obvious options and finally got back to me when he remembered it. One more or less collateral victim didn't matter in the general scheme of things, I suppose, and the larger objective had to be served. Flory might have been an evil-minded fuckbag who enjoyed sucker-punching people, but I couldn't help thinking that he'd have been more use to us alive than dead. Never mind. I had an ace up my sleeve that might be almost as good.

I had no idea where he lived, of course, which was a bit of a bugger when it came to tracking the man down. Without his students, the martial arts club was a goner, too. I had a name, a description and a reasonable profile to work with, and one lead that might help. Michael put me on to Martin, but was much too curious about why I wanted a word, and Martin was nowhere to be found when I looked where Michael sent me. That meant taking time off work to go hunting rather than being able to multitask it concurrently with the supply runs. This must have been part of the test as far as the bad guys were concerned – making sure I had a brain to back up the brawn. My quarry wasn't in the phone book, so all I could do was hope he registered to vote. The electoral roll took a lot of searching, working borough by borough, but my eighth town hall finally yielded a possibility. That had taken two days, and there were more boroughs to check, so I had to decide whether to go straight for this one or check the rest.

I compromised, finishing the afternoon with another records search and deciding to check the address I had that evening. I sat in an alleyway opposite a dismal flat in Holloway all night, only to see a tweedy little man leave for work in the morning. I watched him through the stair windows as he walked out of the right-hand door and down to street level, but his movements were wrong to be the man I wanted – plus his height was wrong and he didn't move like a man disguising that. Nothing in the file said Flory was trained to move in disguise anyway, so it seemed like a non-starter. Add that to a flat whose door was easily observed and we were clearly in the wrong territory. I picked his pocket on the off-chance, just to be sure, and there was a driving licence whose photo corroborated my wasted time.

I cleaned up in a West End Gents toilet and went back to the search. Day four gave me another suspect near Wanstead Flats in the East End, and also saw me finish my sweep of the capital. Either this was the man I wanted, he lived outside London or he was a very naughty boy for dodging his legal obligation to register the address at which he resided.

This address looked more likely. A solid front door in a house converted into two flats and the possibility was upstairs, so he had a reasonable defensive position in there. Thick curtains on the window, it seemed, since the only hint of light was from a loose edge on one side. I settled in to wait for movement.

By eleven o'clock there was not a single sign of life, and I was getting bored. I was sick of all the dicking around, too, and wanted this over and done with so I could get on with the larger job at hand. There's a time to wait and a time to act, and if I wanted to get anywhere with this I might as well act.

Graeme's doorbell made no sound to the outside world, and the door muffled whatever noises I might have heard from within. The spyhole stayed dark, too. I rang the bell again, the nervous expression I was wearing becoming a touch irritable as though I was in a hurry – if he had any sense there'd be a camera hooked up around here somewhere and waiting for him to answer the door would have fluffed the performance before it began. I was going to have to pitch this right if I wanted it to work anyway.

The door opened as I was ringing for the third time. 'John? What the fuck are you doing here?' Graeme didn't exactly look delighted to see me. 'How did you—'

'No time. Just let me in, will you? The plod have been sniffing round my place.'

That got his attention. After a moment of indecision, the fool let me in and led me upstairs. Not another word was spoken until we were safely out of the hallway and inside his flat.

'What about the plod? And what made you think of coming here?'

'Because if it's about the you-know-what, you and Martin will be as stuffed as me.'

'Right.' Now he looked really unhappy. 'Tell you what, sit down a minute and I'll put the kettle on, then we can sort out what to do.' I moved to a chair and sat while Graeme left the room, then bounced right back up and followed him quietly to the kitchen. He was reaching into a drawer as the kettle boiled, despite all the necessary tea things being sat on the counter, and as my arm closed around his neck I caught sight of the Browning automatic he'd been after.

'Bad puppy,' I whispered as he struggled. 'No biscuit.' A few more seconds and he went limp, the chokehold having done its work.

Cable ties at his wrists and ankles, a check of his pockets, emptying them into a plastic bag. All gloved, of course – as I'd been since before ringing the bell. I wanted this to be nice and clean. A gag improvised from clean socks and some gaffer tape to keep him quiet if he came round while I took his car keys and went looking for a vehicle. The helpful sod only had an estate, so it was simply a matter of wrapping him in a rug and carrying him over my shoulder. It's a classic.

By one o'clock we were in my lock-up, which was roomy enough for Graeme's car to sit inside while I worked. Graeme had come round while we were in transit, so I'd had to subdue him again to unload him. By the time he came round again, I had him fixed to a framework that held him standing with his arms out, angled a little forward. Just the way I needed him.

'Hello, Graeme,' I said, facing his open hostility with a smile. 'I'm afraid you're fucked, mate.' He tried to reply, but the gag stopped him. This was a much more solid affair than my improvised job, holding his tongue down with a plate inside the mouth and his jaw closed with a series of straps that ran over his skull. I'd discovered the design during a previous job, and a specialist S&M website had been kind enough to supply one, complete with next-day delivery. 'You see, Graeme, your masters have come to the conclusion that you've been telling tales out of class and think you should be prevented from doing so any more. To that effect, I've been asked to make sure you never tell anyone anything ever again. Now, they didn't specify whether they just meant this world or if they wanted me to cover any post-mortem interrogation, so I've decided to make doubly sure that you won't be coming back to give me grief once I've taken your place.' Graeme's eyes betrayed a perfectly understandable level of fear, especially once I rolled out my instrument tray and pulled the cover off.

'You're lucky in one respect, Graeme. What I'm about to do will be a lot easier for me if you're unconscious.' With that I applied a little pressure somewhere useful, and Graeme's eyes closed.

I started with the mouth. Removing the gag, I used dental callipers to hold Graeme's jaw open, then reached in with my scalpel and started to slice quickly through his tongue. I'd been practising this with a cow tongue from the butcher, so I was ready for what my knife would hit. There was a lot of blood as the blade worked its way through, and I was glad to get in there with a hot iron bar to cauterise the wound. A moan of pain rolled out of Graeme's throat even through his unconsciousness, and once the bleeding was properly staunched I had to pause to check his vitals and make sure he didn't go into shock. Much as

I would have liked to end it there, I still had work to do that needed him to be alive.

I was covered in blood, the dark-red fluid sprayed down the front of my white suit and across my facemask – it was a good thing I'd chosen a full-face polycarbonate one rather than those silly paper things that only cover the nose and mouth. I stopped for a moment to wash myself down a bit and throw a little sawdust on the floor to reduce the chance of slipping in the mess I'd made.

With my gloves and visor clean again, I went back to work. The smell was thick in the air, hot and metallic with blood as if I'd had my nose broken, but with a hint of fried bacon under it. The suit was hot, too, and I could feel the sweat trickling down my back as I picked up needle and thread to secure Graeme's mouth. Slow and steady, each stitch individually tied off with the right incantation to ensure he wouldn't be able to communicate from the other side. Methodical work is the secret of a good ritual, after all.

Next was an easier section. I had set up a brazier in the corner, which was one of the reasons why I was sweating so much in the suit. The fact that the suit didn't breathe really wasn't helping matters, since the suit's hood was up and only my face was exposed to air behind the face shield. A smear of petroleum jelly across my eyebrows kept the sweat out of my eyes, but it ran down over my face as I pulled on a pair of welding gauntlets and reached for the axe with its red-hot blade. The hands were the next things to go: left then right, since he was a southpaw, with an incantation for each. Now he would be unable to move anything from the other side.

The smell from that was overwhelming. I had to stop for a moment so I could be sick, then turned off the brazier and dropped the axe in a bucket of cold water. I was almost two hours in by this point and still not finished, but Graeme's decision to wake up was, I suppose, an unavoidable delay. Another touch to his neck and he slipped back under, putting an end to the hysterical attempts at screaming.

At least I was into the home stretch. My next tool was a crochet hook, from a friendly haberdashery that thought I was buying it for my wife – if only they knew, eh?

The human eye is held in place by a membrane called the conjunctiva, and it took a very careful hand to cut through that without damaging the eyeball underneath. That was far too valuable to me for any harm to befall it. Next came the muscles that move the eyeball about. There are six of those, and the crochet hook slipped around to reach them nicely. A gentle pull to expose them, then slice through each muscle in turn with a small scalpel. After the last one, you can lever the eyeball clear and sever the optic nerve. Once that was done, I dropped it into a bowl and repeated the process on the other side. Finally it was time for more stitches, and the eye is a clean enough unit that I didn't have to waste time washing up to keep grip. Again the stitching, again the incantations, again the sealing off from any contact after death. I poured hot wax into one ear, marking it with a seal and an incantation to close it off for ever. The other, however, had to wait.

As did I. I needed Graeme conscious for the next phase, so once I'd finished preparing the incense, placed it around him and the spot I would be working from and set it to smoking, I took time out to vomit up what was left of my stomach contents.

He came round after about ten minutes, grunting in pain and disorientated as hell. I couldn't even begin to imagine what he was going through, and really didn't want to since it wasn't going to help my concentration. I simply took my place in the empty circle, pronounced some Latin from a very unpleasant book, focused my mind on the eagle seal I'd seen on the package and swallowed an eyeball whole.

The images came so fiercely that somewhere a million miles away my body staggered. A group of twelve in a circle, Graeme presumably being the thirteenth, all masked and enacting some kind of ritual that seemed very similar to raising the dead. Michael's face, brow furrowed in concentration. A portrait of Hitler, the group all raising their arms in that classic salute. A register of births. A register of deaths. Folkestone laughing while a group of men sang around him. A plan of what looked like a castle lying next to a map. Then darkness.

I was back in my body, and Graeme had blacked out again. I started to clean up, getting things ready for my departure.

Everything was prepared when Graeme came back. My penultimate act was to whisper a fond farewell.

'You know what, Graeme? I know it wasn't your fault that things went wrong. It was mine. I fucked your plan, and your life, and now I'm going to wipe all trace of your nasty friends from the face of the Earth. You're just a fucking job to me, asshole. Another type of vermin to be exterminated. And do you know why I'm telling you all this? Because I've made sure that you won't be able to tell anyone else for the rest of time. You'll just get to think about how badly I fucked you while you burn in Hell, or whatever spiritual septic tank shit like you ends up in. Enjoy it, asshole – you earned every moment.'

Then I sealed the ear, and walked away to the sound of his mute screaming.

At the door, I looked back around the space to make sure I'd got everything right. Powder covered the floor and all the worktops, and wicks led between the two. I checked outside to make sure the coast was clear, then pushed the door open just wide enough to get through. Off came the face shield, suit, gloves and boots, all of which went back inside. On went my shoes, covered with plastic supermarket bags to protect me a little further. Finally I pulled out a lighter, opened the top, sparked the wick, threw it inside and walked quickly towards the road. I was wearing the same disguise that had hired the garage and once the bags came off my feet and went into my pocket there was nothing to mark me out against the rest of society, had any of it been walking around at five in the morning. Behind me was a bright white light, leaking around the edges of the lock-up's door.

Thermite's amazing. A compound of simple powdered metals, it burns at an incredible temperature that removes all sorts of annoying forensic traces. It melts human flesh and bones, turns most metals to slag and in this case boiled my sweat and vomit beyond recognition while making sure that all they'd find of Graeme Flory was an empty flat. Only two people would ever know what had happened in that place, and one of us wasn't ever going to be in a position to tell.

Me, I'd just have to live with it. God help me.

Chapter Ten

I've pulled some shit in my time, but that had to have been the single worst night of my life. By the time I arrived home the sun was coming up and it was all I could do to get to the toilet in time for a series of dry heaves that left my throat raw and my head spinning. Post-magic comedown had never been that bad for me before, and I couldn't help wondering what sort of price I was going to end up paying for what I'd done to Graeme. These things are a piece of piss to order, and not so bad to plan if you can hide from the objective behind hopes of a last-minute escape, but actually performing the act changes it from theory into a practice worse than the description could ever be.

I called in sick, crawled into bed and slept as only the exhausted can. My dreams were filled with Graeme's face, but he had company. Sophie was there, wearing the confused expression she'd had when she died, and behind her followed a parade of people I'd killed over the years. It was a classic guilt dream, just my subconscious trying to rearrange itself so that what I'd done wouldn't snap my mind into little pieces. The human survival instinct is strong, and we can cope with an amazing amount of really bad stuff as long as we can find a way to process it. Mine was duty, the fact that things like this had to happen occasionally and that almost all of the people they happened to were bad people. The odd civilian might wander into the net from time to time, but the lives I'd taken were a tiny fraction of the lives I'd saved. Sometimes I look forward to it, to removing a particularly nasty piece of work from the world, but on the whole it's just business. I don't enjoy that part of the job – in fact, I don't really enjoy any part of my job – but I wouldn't ask anyone to take my place. I'm just enough of a bastard to survive this, but even I have moments when I don't want to look in the mirror.

I awoke to the sound of the doorbell. Folkestone was there, looking at me with a certain amount of sadistic amusement. I must have looked pretty damned awful to get a grin like that out of him.

'We heard that you'd called in sick.'

'Yeah. Not feeling so good – had a late night.'

'So it's done, then?'

'Yeah, it's done.'

'Good.'

That seemed to be the end of it. Folkestone was gone as suddenly as he'd arrived and I sat down to watch TV while I tried to work out what time it was. The news was on, reporting the rather unsuccessful attempts of the Fire Brigade to put out my fire in the lock-up. One of the reasons I used thermite was its resistance to extinguishing methods, meaning that all the evidence would be destroyed despite everyone's best efforts to save what was inside. Scotland Yard were calling it a terrorist bomb factory and theorising that some kind of accident had caused the fire. I'd heard worse cover-ups but couldn't help wondering which side had put this one in place.

The weekend passed and I found a little comfort in Sarah. It was the usual thing for us: dinner, drinks and sex. The plan was supposed to be no strings attached, but on the Saturday night I caught her looking at me a little differently.

'What's wrong?' she asked.

'Just work.'

'I thought we were leaving our jobs at the door.'

'Yeah. It's just a little stressful at the moment, y'know?'

'Do you want to talk about it?'

'Can't.' If only she knew.

She wrapped her arms around me, holding me close so I could smell her hair – a combination of expensive shampoo and fresh sweat. Her skin was warm on mine and it was good to just close my eyes and relax for a little while.

'It's going to be fine, John,' she said. 'Hey, how about we go away for a few days when you've finished whatever this is?'

'Sure.' Like I was going to have time – between the cover job, the real job and the demands the bad guys were making on me it was a wonder I found time to wipe my backside, much less sneak in a dirty weekend. 'That'll be nice.'

'Yeah, I thought so. Where do you fancy going?'

'Pick somewhere nice – surprise me.'

Monday came, and I went back to work, claiming a cold while everyone thought I'd taken a long weekend. Michael was pleased to see me, and was looking at me in a whole different way, so I assumed he'd heard that Graeme had been taken care of. Apparently I was to be ready for a meeting the next night, and Folkestone would once again be collecting me.

Which was exactly what happened. There was the same nonsense with the bag, and I was taken to a similar room, this time hung with banners that had the eagle symbol embroidered on them. There was a desk, behind which sat Mr Gold, and a chair for me. He motioned for me to sit.

'We're very pleased with what you've done, Mr Dennis. Flory is obviously dead, but despite our very best efforts we've been unable to compel him to communicate. How did you achieve this?'

'The "Closing Off" ritual. Shutting down each sense one by one and sealing the orifices before death.'

'That explains the time you took in preparation. Some of us were wondering whether you were going to go through with it.' So had I, but that wasn't important.

'I wanted to be sure that it was done properly. I was told to ensure that he never communicated again, and that's a pretty major job.'

'Quite.' A moment's pause as Gold looked at me, considering my actions and filing them in his opinion of me. Perhaps he hadn't thought I could be quite so ruthless, or that there'd be more clearing up to do. Maybe he really had thought that I'd bottled it completely. There was no way to tell. 'We have decided to accept you as a member of the group. Your duties will be as follows: firstly, you will take part in all rituals, occupying the place that should be held by Michael. It was his father's place and it is right that he inherit it, but he is not ready to do so. Secondly, you will tutor Michael in the arts to make him ready to step forward. We estimate that this will take at least another two years, after which a new place will be found for you, perhaps within the circle itself. There may be other functions for you to perform, in accordance with our greater objectives. These objectives may or may not be revealed to you in time, but I expect you to remember your place and not ask questions whose answers you are not authorised to know. We are working to rebuild society here, to make it better again – we seek to cure the sickness that has grown in the British people and lead them back to their rightful place in the world. Your services and assistance will not be forgotten when that is done, and I can assure you that the rewards will be more than moral. Do you understand these terms?'

'I do.'

'And do you agree to them?'

'I do.'

'Then you will be initiated this evening. Folkestone will take you to change.'

'You've got clothes for me?'

'Oh yes, Mr Dennis. We've had your measure for some time.'

Folkestone did indeed take me to a small room where black trousers, boots and tie waited, along with a crisp white shirt. They must have checked my sizes when they searched my flat, since everything fitted perfectly. Creases were immaculate and the boots shined to a mirror finish, just like a military uniform, and I started to have a bad feeling about what might complete the outfit. Everything was expensive, though, tailored in good-quality materials way above what you'd find commercially – obviously they had a tailor who knew how to keep his mouth shut. I checked everything in the mirror, and had to admit that I looked good. My hair was still short and completed the picture just a little too well.

After a few more minutes, Folkestone returned with a small bag. Indicating that I should turn away, he reached into the bag and pulled out a length of rope, which he used to secure my hands. Next he fitted a pair of goggles over my head, checked the fit and flicked a switch on the side. My world went black as shutters closed across the lenses, leaving me in a position that wasn't exactly comfortable.

Of course, that was all standard initiation practice. It didn't mean I liked being handicapped around someone like Folkestone.

Off we went – out of the room, along a corridor and finally to a stop. There was a knocking and a creak as a door opened.

'State your name.' Was this meant for me? I had to assume so.

'John Dennis.'

'Enter, John Dennis. It is your time.' A hand took me by the arm and led me forward a few steps, presumably into the centre of wherever we were doing the thing. 'You stand in darkness, John Dennis. But soon shall you see the light. You stand in bondage, but soon shall you be free. You stand in supplication, but soon shall you stand with us. Are these the things you desire?'

'They are.' I didn't understand why this group insisted on having me wing my responses, but at least they were keeping it easy. Most of the time you get a period of training before acceptance, and the lines needed for initiation are part of that. Still, when in Rome . . .

'You have shown that you are worthy, in heart, mind and deed. We have examined you, and found you suitable to stand among us. Now hear the secret history of the world, and learn your true place in it.'

Oh boy, it was lecture time.

'Once we were great. The might of our people stretched across the globe, and a whim in one place became a command far away. The source of our strength was in leadership, obedience and discipline, and through those means we wielded power in this world and all the others.' The goggles snapped open to reveal a man standing before me in the robes I'd seen before. Behind him hovered the image of a globe with an eagle above it, wings spread as if to shade it from the sun. It was a pretty impressive piece of 3D work, and the tinge surrounding everything told me that I was wearing tinted goggles that would let me see things depending on colour. This wasn't the first time I'd worn a pair and they're actually a pretty nifty piece of kit – fantastic for watching old B-movies, too.

'Then came the wars—' more narration '—and within conflict we found greater discipline. The peoples of our empire worked together and defeated a terrible foe. Our fallen enemy's land became decadent and mad; there was chaos, depravity and ruin. In spite of this, that land found a new leader – terrible in his power, strong in discipline and supported by those who would see themselves restored to supremacy. That nation rose to fight again, and we in our complacency allowed it. That next war was as terrible as the first, and our victory came at too high a price. While our defeated enemy found new strength of purpose in ruin, we became decadent ourselves. Our empire fell about us, lost in foolishness and poor leadership.' The image changed, the eagle's head now hanging low beside drooping wings. The coloured lenses in my goggles must have been switched around to show the new image. 'We have set ourselves to renew that lost strength, to rebuild our empire, to bring our nation back into the light. It is no easy task that we have set ourselves, and the challenge is vast, yet we stand ready. Will you stand with us?'

'I will.' The goggles went black again, and I was turned to the right. When they reopened I was facing a painting of Britannia, the goggles bringing out details that aren't in the traditional version. This one showed armies butchering men, women and children behind her.

'The cost of our resurrection will be great, and blood will be part of that price. Your actions have shown strength in the face of this need, but will you hold to that strength? Will you use it to promote our ends, to fight for our place in the world, to cut away that which is weak, both inside yourself and in the world at large?'

'I will.' Out went the lights, and another turn to the right. The next view was a tapestry that would have given Hieronymus Bosch nightmares. People were doing things to each other that looked downright impossible; there was cannibalism, rape, murder and all sorts of other unpleasantness.

'This is the price of our failure: a descent into madness and horror. We are already on the path to this fate, yet we may still avert it if we are strong. We must eschew despair and embrace courage. Have you that courage? Can you stand before the abyss and turn it back? Will you use that courage to remain true to our beliefs, in service to our noble goal and the interests of your countrymen?'

'I will.' And another blind turn to the right. I was now looking at a view of paradise. People were laughing, singing and enjoying themselves, children were at play, the factories were at work and all seemed right with the world. Every single face was white, of course – there was no place for Johnny Foreigner in this paradise. The only blot on that perfectly Aryan landscape was the men in black standing watching them at points across the picture – overseers making sure that everyone was happy, whether they wanted to be or not.

'This is the world we seek to build. A world where men and women are safe and healthy, where the worker is rewarded for his honest toil and mothers may raise their children safely. A world where crime no longer exists, and all the people strive together to spread that enlightenment and empire across the globe. Will you hold this vision in your heart? Will you make it your credo, and draw strength from its joy? Will you take courage from the nobility of our cause, even as we walk through chaos to achieve it?'

'I will.' One more turn to the right, shades down once again, then my hands were untied.

'You were told that we would free you, and now we shall.' Someone was slipping a jacket onto me, over my arms and shoulders, then buttoning the front. A belt went around my waist, and a strap over my shoulder. 'You were told that you would see the light, and now you shall.' The goggles came off, and Mr Gold was standing in front of me in a black uniform, rank marks shining on his lapels and an eagle on his armband and the front of his hat. The same eagle stood behind him, four feet high and glittering with gold. He was holding another hat, which he passed to me. 'You were told that you would stand with us. Take your last oath and do so.

'Do you swear unswerving loyalty to this society? Do you swear unconditional obedience to our leader and to the leaders that he determines for you?'

'I do.'

'Then welcome.' He stepped forward and shook my hand, as did the other eleven men who had watched from outside my restricted field of vision, each in their turn. There was back-slapping and congratulations, and all the usual palaver that goes with the end of an initiation. I was now officially one of the team.

We left the room, whose decorations had already been folded away to leave nothing but the gold eagle, and proceeded into the next room. There was another group waiting for us, all of them wearing the same uniform with varying degrees of success. Military uniforms are basically designed for a particular type of body shape, and while they look good on my six-foot-one, well-exercised frame they don't really work when you're five-foot-eight and shaped like a fruit. Take a look at Himmler sometime, or compare Goering's look in the First and Second World Wars and you'll see what I mean. Fat blokes in uniform just don't look right. I was introduced properly to a succession of people, whose names I noted very carefully, and made to feel even more welcome. Drinks were served, and I thought I caught the flash of a face I recognised. No chance to track them, though, since everyone wanted to greet the new member and offer whatever support they could. I was going to have a good month at the office if half the offers came true.

The evening wore down after a time, after talk of politics and money – both from very practical angles, since these were people who actually *had* power, rather than the types who just sit in pubs and dream. Folkestone, also in uniform, came to tell me that he was ready to drive me home whenever I was ready. It seemed like a good idea, so I started to make my excuses and head towards the door.

I was almost gone when someone called me back. 'I don't think you've met Miss Gentle, have you?' I turned and saw the face I thought I'd glimpsed before. A familiar face from other places. Someone who knew me by a different name. 'This is John Dennis, our new recruit. Mr Dennis, this is Alexandra Gentle.'

'A pleasure to meet you, Miss Gentle.' At least we were both using different names.

'Likewise, Mr Dennis.' Her cool blue eyes matched mine, and the gaze held for a fraction of a second longer than might have been considered proper for a first meeting. Of all the people I'd thought there was a danger of running into on a job, I was not expecting Miss Penelope Marsh of the Security Service, better known as MI5.

I got my ass the fuck out of there as fast as I could.

Chapter Eleven

I was allowed to leave without a bag on my head, and we turned out to have been underneath an old building in the City. Not really a surprise, but it was nice to have an address to go with all the other information I'd gained that evening. The drive home was a tense one, though. I was expecting Folkestone's mobile phone to ring at any second with orders to bring me back or simply take me out on the spot.

What in hell's name was Penny Marsh doing there? I could only hope that her use of a different name was a sign that she was working the group for MI5, but that in itself was a potential problem. If she was there officially, that meant she had handlers, contacts and all sorts of weak points that might get me blown. She was bound to report my appearance, which might well turn into a shit-storm between departments. She was under the impression that I worked for the Army's 14th Intelligence Detachment and I was quite sure that she didn't know my real name. What if she thought my current cover was really me? The Det wouldn't admit to having anyone by my name, since it didn't, and would certainly deny having anyone investigating the Eagle Society since, again, it didn't – at least as far as I knew. And that was just working from the assumption that she was there officially. If she was there as an actual member, I was royally screwed – she'd give me up out of loyalty and then the whole bloody edifice would come crashing down.

The question, then, was how to proceed. Did I carry on as if everything was normal? Wrap the whole thing up, arrest everyone we could and hope for the best? Eliminate Miss Marsh? I was going to have to report the contact, that was for sure, and then the Boss would have a decision to make. I had no misconceptions about my own expendability in a situation like this, but was really rather keen on staying alive just a little longer. Assuming I had any kind of input, of course.

There was also the question of reporting. I was going to have to sweep my flat for bugs while trying not to look like I was doing it, just in case there were cameras. I had some shopping to do. The next evening was spent in a very expensive shop in Mayfair, the kind of place where paranoid businessmen go to buy armoured trench coats that make them feel like spies, and where security consultants send their clients for a nice little kickback. Knowing what I wanted saved me quite a few quid, as did the ability to talk about it knowledgeably with a guy who'd lost a finger during some private work in sunnier climes. We ended up swapping jokes, and I spun him a tale of not-so-derring-do that had him chuckling merrily. By the time I left they had me filed as yet another private contractor, the sort that they make a living forgetting all about until you walk in the door again – and even then they can be wonderfully shaky about your name.

Sweeping the flat then became much easier. I replaced my landline telephone with a new model that had a built-in line resistance meter for checking to see if anything was attached to my connection that shouldn't have been there – a really efficient way to bug someone, since the unit draws power from the line and doesn't need to transmit a radio signal to get its information home. It was also a nicely innocuous way to start – there was nothing inherently suspicious about a new telephone, after all. There was nothing on the line, and if there was anything in the telephone itself it was now disconnected from the outside world and on its way to the bin. I changed the phone in the bedroom, too, for another metered type. Again, that would stop anything in the original unit, but it would also let me monitor the line for anything unexpected while using the phone in there.

Next came checking for radio transmissions. I switched off my mobile phone (a radio transmitter I already knew about) and took a walk around the flat room by room. I wasn't expecting to find any microphones in the living room or bedroom – the phones would have easily been the best place for them, but when the bathroom and kitchen came up clean I was reasonably happy. I don't mind the paranoia, even though the care it leads to can get in the way sometimes. If anyone from the Society asked, my excuse for the sweep was simply that now I'd been initiated, I wanted to cover not only my ass but everyone else's as well. I also needed somewhere secure for Michael's lessons. That explanation wouldn't have worked before, but it was perfect now and if I had been bugged, then I could have made a nice show of reporting back in a terrified manner, which I could see amusing Folkestone no end. There was still the possibility of a burst-transmission unit, one that recorded passively and sent a compressed signal only when a control unit told it to, but I had a little box that would find such devices the moment they started transmitting, record the activation signal and then lead me straight to them. A white-noise generator would keep things confidential in the meantime.

Stage three came when I turned on the computer that sat on my desk for all the world to see. Given that it had its own connection to the outside world, I would have considered it an ideal place for a monitoring device that could combine micro-phone, keystroke logger, email reader and web-history recorder that just squirted information out in the background. A software scan came up clean, and a look inside the case didn't reveal any surprises. I logged into the router and found that all was well there, too.

Finally I felt safe enough to pull out the laptop from its current hiding place in the bottom of the wardrobe. Another scan here showed a clean bill of health, so after three solid hours of searching I was finally comfortable with the idea of firing up the white noise and putting in a report. That didn't stop me from playing some music to cover the sound of my keystrokes, of course, but that was as much habit as it was paranoia.

I made my drop the next morning – two hours' worth of typing, racking my brains for more details and typing some more, over and over until I finally ran out of details. Names, descriptions, the address of where we'd been, details of the ritual, imagery and uniforms, even down to the car that Folkestone had driven me home in. I also added a warning about Miss Marsh's involvement. If something was about to go wrong I wanted to be sure that the Boss knew everything there was to know about these people, so they could be rolled up after I'd gone. It might take some time, but people with that much influence and an agenda to mess with government were a definite danger that needed to be removed. If I didn't do it, someone else would.

Back at the bank, Michael was very pleased with himself, and quite happy to let me in on the joke. He was on the Society's ruling Council, it transpired, even if he wasn't qualified to fulfil his magical duties, and he made sure I knew who was in charge. He seemed happy about everything except the lessons I was supposed to give him – he didn't have much interest in that side of things and was more focused on the rewards of his position than the responsibilities, which explained why he hadn't been at my initiation. That was fine by me, since it would keep me right where I wanted to be long enough to arrange for things to be taken care of in a suitable fashion. Michael wasn't ever going to take his place in that circle, since it would be gone long before he even came close to being ready for it.

Michael did have one instruction for me, something that had apparently come from our leader: Sarah had to go. The Society had checked her background, and it turned out that her maternal grandmother was Jewish. 'I know she's been keeping you entertained, John, but it won't do. Even if it's just been a matter of screwing her, you'll have to get rid. OK?'

'Right. Can't have it. Bloody Jews get everywhere, don't they?'

'Don't they just. But not for much longer, of course.' Michael's grin was sickening. He was sharing a secret with a trusted compatriot, someone who saw the world as he did. No need to keep the civilised mask on when it was just us. But there was also an opportunity here.

'What about the Gentle woman, then? Is she single?'

'Pah! She's carved out of ice. God knows I've tried my luck, but she's not having any of it. Dinner, flowers, champagne – she's immune to all of it. I wouldn't be surprised to find that her knickers are glued on permanently. She's a good little soldier, but might as well be a nun.'

'Damn, I thought she was giving me the eye last night.'

'I doubt it. I've got a sneaking suspicion that she might be a closet dyke. Hmm, maybe I could threaten to out her, blackmail her into bed . . .' It was just the kind of shitty thing I'd expect Michael to say, but I wanted to slap him anyway.

'Still, I might give it a shot.'

'Well, be careful. The Society doesn't exactly approve of random fucking among the membership, so keep it quiet unless you're actually going to make a decent effort with her. Come clubbing with me at the weekend instead. If we grab a packet of Charlie on the way out we'll have no problem getting as many sluts as we want.' Michael wasn't going to give Casanova any worries, but he had sparked an idea about how to make contact with Miss Marsh. Perhaps a touch of apparent romance would be the way to give us time alone.

I made some discreet enquiries at the next meeting of the circle. There were plans underway for a big ritual, something to do with the greater goals of changing government and putting the leader we wanted into position – apparently I'd be told more at a later date. Sir James, formerly Mr Gold, seemed interested in my reasons, since Miss Marsh – Gentle – had expressed a similar interest after my departure. 'I told her you were single. That is correct, isn't it?'

'It is now, yes. Michael was kind enough to let me know about the woman I was seeing.'

'Good. We don't want to go mixing with that sort. You're an obvious specimen of good breeding and I'm sure you want to keep any offspring that way. Perhaps we might see about arranging for you and Miss Gentle to get to know each other a little better. She's a very nice girl, you know.' Oh great, they were into eugenics as well. Of course a pair of blond-haired, blue-eyed types would seem like a good match: we could have little *Übermenschen* babies together and build an Aryan paradise for them from the corpses of our enemies. What joy.

But to leave the field clear for my new *amore*, there was an administrative matter that required my attention. Timing was the issue here, and location – a place out of the way to give room for any unpleasantness to remain discreet, or somewhere public to keep a lid on it? It's an age-old question that people have asked themselves over the years, not just in my profession but in every walk of life. It was time to dump Sarah. Picking the spot was going to be tricky – in private it was most likely to be immediately pre- or post-sex, neither of which were good, and if she flew off in public then I'd have a whole different set of troubles. In the end I found a quiet little restaurant that didn't know either of us and didn't seem to contain any faces that I'd seen before.

'What's wrong?' Sarah asked. I'd been quiet since we met up for the evening and the look of concern on her face spoke volumes about why I really should have thought about doing this sooner off my own bat. 'Is it still work?'

'I don't think I'm going to be able to see you any more.' I said. There was no way around it any longer. She'd nailed me with the question and all I could do was bite the bullet and tell her the truth.

'What?'

'The way work's going and with everything else, I just don't think it's fair on you.'

'Isn't that my decision?' She was obviously not happy. I had clearly chosen the wrong tack. 'I mean, don't I get a say in whether I think you're treating me unfairly? If I thought you were, you'd bloody well know it.'

'Of course you get a say, but I keep feeling bad about having to run off and leave you. I hate the way we don't see each other for ages and then when we do there's this whole other thing going on. I know this was just supposed to be sex, but—'

'I know.'

'Exactly. I've broken the rules and you don't need the mess.'

'What if I had as well?'

'What?'

'Look, stupid, if you're trying to dump me because you've started to get more involved, what would you say if I told you that I felt the same way?'

'Um?' This wasn't the reaction I was expecting.

'You really are a moron sometimes, aren't you?' She smiled. 'You're trying to break this off because you're getting involved emotionally, right? Well, I know we said that that was out of bounds but the truth is . . . well . . . I've broken the rules, too.'

The penny dropped. Crap. Crap, crap, crappity-crap.

'So you're saying that—'

'Yeah, I feel the same way.' No she bloody didn't, but I couldn't exactly say that.

'Oh.'

'So how about we change the rules and see what happens?'

'I'm still not sure that's such a good idea.'

'Why not?'

'Well, there's work, and—'

'Fuck work. Give me a real reason.'

'I'm not sure that I really want to be in a full-on relationship right now.'

'Why not? What's to stop us giving it a try?'

'Look, Sarah—'

'Don't you "Look, Sarah" me. What's wrong with the idea of us taking it a step further? You prefer just having me as a blow-up doll or something? Jesus, this is why I was so cagey about letting on – I should have known you'd be just like every other wanker I've been out with!' Her voice was still low, but the anger was palpable and the look she was giving me could have curdled milk. 'It's hard enough trying to find someone without having them turn out to be a shit the moment you risk opening up to them. Look, you're scared of commitment. Well, you know what – so am I. Do you know how hard it's been for me to deal with what's happening here? All I wanted was someone to scratch an itch and then I messed up by falling for you. So I kept it quiet, hoping you'd start to feel the same and we could make something out of this. But no, you have to be an asshole and run away when what we've actually got is exactly what we both secretly wanted. What the hell is wrong with you?'

'Sarah, there are things … stuff I can't talk about. My time with the Army …' That was a cheap shot, but I was running out of options. There wasn't really much of a way back from here and we both knew it. The smart thing for us both would have been to stop right there and walk away, but for some reason I couldn't do it. I wanted to be somewhere else, but my legs wouldn't pick me up, so I just kept sitting there offering excuses like an idiot.

'We can work through that, can't we?'

'Sarah—'

'No, I suppose we can't, then. You're a fucking idiot, John, you really are. And someday you're going to realise that. One day you're going to look back on tonight and realise that you threw away a good thing, and you're going to hate yourself even more than you do now. You don't need a girlfriend, you need a fucking shrink.'

Not my finest hour, but if you can't take a joke, you shouldn't sign up. The priority was to woo Miss Marsh and get her back to my flat, which had the advantage of being secure from monitoring. I had to find out what she was up to before I could plan my next step and there seemed no better way than asking her just what the hell she thought she was up to.

I had to wait another three weeks for that introduction, at the next monthly meeting. In the meantime I worked, tried to get some information into Michael's head despite his best efforts to prevent it from taking root, and did my part in preparation for the upcoming ritual. My job was to check the area around the proposed ritual site and make sure that Folkestone and his storm-troopers could keep it secure while we were waving our wands about. This meant I had to work with Folkestone, and it was an interesting experience to say the least. He was fascinated by what I'd done to Graeme, not from a magical point of view but with the actual methods. He asked me to describe removing his eyes over and over again, as though he were memorising the technique, and giggled about the thermite. This was not the best way to become my friend, and it started grating on me pretty quickly. By the end of our third visit to the site I was very glad to see the back of him. He was smart, though: I'd seen it in his eyes. He was the kind of man who enjoys finding new ways to cause pain, and I could see him taking his time over a victim, that mind creating new ways to hurt as he enacted them and enjoyed the results.

My report went down well, that the stately home we were planning to use was secure and suitable for our purposes. The section of the grounds chosen was free of places where an observer could hide, and Folkestone's team would be able to patrol without disturbing us while we worked. Preparations had also begun, we were told, to get the necessary equipment into position and dress the site appropriately. Banners, incense burners and altar were all ready for use whenever it was decided that the time was right. That time, according to the astrologer, was the following Thursday night, so everyone agreed that the best policy was to take over the house for the entire week and use the time for training and indoctrination of the troops. It would also give me an opportunity to get to know some of the troops personally, it was suggested, since part of my remit was going to involve working with them in the future. Everyone was to attend, which meant that I might well be about to get my chance with Miss Marsh.

Chapter Twelve

Austen Hall was a big old stately pile in the country, very much like the dump that the Service uses for training recruits. Lots of rooms, gardens you could hide an army in and loads of famous dead people on the walls. Apparently it belonged to some industrialist with sympathies in the Eagle Society's direction, and the old duffer had kindly allowed us to borrow it for the week – even to the point of sending the entire staff on holiday while we were there.

By the time I got there, Folkestone and his minions already had the place up and running. Rooms had been assigned for officers, with shared accommodation for the ranks and female staff. I was lucky enough to have a room to myself but Miss Marsh was going to be stuck in with someone else as part of a mutual chaperoning deal, and that might cause a problem. Somehow we were going to have to work out a way of getting some time alone to discuss what was going on. I still needed to find out exactly what she was planning and how it might affect my own operation.

Of course, it wasn't going to be easy. I saw her a couple of times in passing when I arrived on the Friday, but there was no chance for me to talk to her as she was accompanied by one of the older women, a stern-looking battleaxe who probably wouldn't have approved of any naughtiness. Saturday passed in drill, meditations and lectures on political theory, but at least there was a social that evening and with it a chance to make contact.

My first plan was to try for a walk on the terrace, but the pouring rain got in the way of that. Next was an attempt at dancing, but even though I had no doubt regarding her ability to take my eye out with her high heels, she hadn't a clue how to make those heels waltz – we had to concentrate on avoiding each other's toes to such an extent that conversation wasn't practical. Every time I got close to ducking into a side room with her there was someone in the way, and by the end of the evening there was enough frustration building up between the two of us that we didn't have to act the part of a thwarted couple.

Sunday morning brought a 'group meditation', where the entire company assembled and confirmed its collective intention to make the world a better place. I wasn't entirely sure who it would be better *for*, but that didn't stop me from joining in with the love. The afternoon was theoretically our own free time, but the best I managed was an hour talking to Miss Marsh about nothing while various passing eyeballs made sure we didn't get up to any hanky-panky.

An unexpected break came over dinner on Sunday, when an older woman approached me for a quiet chat.

'I see you've taken a bit of a shine to Miss Gentle,' she said. 'Do you think it's entirely appropriate?'

'I don't see why not. She hasn't mentioned seeing anyone else, and I'm not involved with anyone at the moment.'

'Well, we know that. But we really don't encourage ... flings among members. Of course, it's all terribly romantic out here, but we're not on holiday, you know.'

'Of course not. It's simply that we've not had much chance to talk before now and the free time gives us an opportunity to get to know one another. I suppose you could say that we're testing the waters, so to speak.'

'Indeed.' She smiled a little at that, but it didn't last long. 'You see, Mr Dennis, there's a concern that if things don't work out then you might have difficulty working together.'

'But we don't—'

'Not at the moment, perhaps. But that might change, depending on her assignment. You understand the problem, of course.'

'Of course. So you're suggesting I should back off?'

'No, but it would be for the best if the two of you were to take it slowly. I assume that your intentions are honourable, so you won't mind a little patience in your courtship. It will make things all the sweeter at the end, I assure you.'

'I'm sure it will.'

'I shall speak to Miss Gentle, then, and see if she returns your interest.'

'Thank you. Thank you very much.'

'Not at all, Mr Dennis. I think Miss Gentle would benefit from a little romance in her life. She seems to have very little outside of her work and that's not at all healthy for a girl her age.'

I felt like I was in a costume drama, but if it worked then I was willing to play along.

Miss Marsh had obviously confirmed her willingness by Tuesday evening, since we spent the evening after dinner talking in the drawing room. We were chaperoned, of course, but it was from a discreet distance that gave us the illusion of some small privacy while we talked about everything except the one subject we needed to discuss. To be honest, I didn't trust the house to be free of bugs even if we did find time to talk alone indoors, so this was about the only kind of conversation we could have until we found a way to be outside together. She turned out to be surprisingly good company, with a taste for music that crossed into mine a fair amount. I knew this already, of course, since I'd broken into her flat – her real flat, that is – a while back. It was still nice to hear her talking about it, though; her eyes lighting up as she was able to be a bit of herself, weaving it into her cover as we left the false details behind and found a way for Jack and Penny to have a conversation in the midst of work. At this rate we might even find a way for us to get along in the outside world.

Wednesday afternoon came around, and it was contrived that we found ourselves with a couple of free hours at the same time. Penny seemed pleased with herself as we walked along the terrace.

'The old bats have decided that we're "suitable", whatever that means.' She didn't seem impressed by the manoeuvring going on around us. 'Still, apparently I'm allowed to take a turn around the gardens with you as long as we don't get fresh.'

'Really? Do you trust me to behave, Miss Gentle?'

'I trust that you'll have more sense than to misbehave here, if that's what you mean. Anywhere else would be a different proposition, most likely.' She grinned and held up an arm for me to take. 'Well then? Care to escort me round the shrubbery?'

At last we'd found time alone. After all the bullshit we'd gone through to get here it seemed a bit anticlimactic, but at least there was a chance for me to find out what in hell was actually going on. Not knowing how long we had, I decided to skip the preamble and get to the meat of the matter as soon as we were clear of the house and any prying eyes that might be watching where my hands went.

'So what the hell are you doing here, Miss Marsh?'

'I might ask you the same thing.'

'I asked first.'

'You don't exist, do you know that? I tried looking you up again after our last meeting and you're not there. Not under any of the names I've ever heard for you. Only as John Dennis. Not even the Det admit you exist, and they've been getting more cooperative in the last year or two.' She was referring to the Army branch she thought I worked for – the cover I generally used when I ended up in a military hospital, which was something that happened much more frequently than I might like.

'That doesn't answer my question, Penny. What are you doing here?'

'Blame yourself.'

'What?'

'After you gave me those terrorists last year, my application for field status got a lot more serious attention. This is my reward – a full case of my own, with backup.'

'Such as?'

'All these people in uniform make it very easy for us to take the group apart now. Imagine what would happen if photos of all these important people became public, photos of them in their pseudo-SS uniforms, marching around and *Sieg Heil*-ing each other. They'd be ruined. So that's our leverage to split this nasty little bunch of bastards up and make sure they behave.' The swearing sounded wrong coming from Penny: her cut-glass accent made the words different, somehow dirtier, and while I don't have a problem with the language it sent a frisson down my spine to hear her using it.

'Photographs?'

'Mm-hmm.'

'Of us, here, doing what we're doing?'

'Mm-hmm.' She looked pleased with herself. 'All cleaned up, nice and tidy. No violence, no nonsense, just a little bit of carefully applied blackmail.'

'Bollocks.'

'What?'

'There's more going on than you think, Penny. You need to hold back and let me deal with this.'

'Why?'

'Trust me.'

'Why?'

'I can't tell you that.'

'No. I can't suspend an operation just because you say so. You might have helped get me here, but you used me all the way while you did it. I don't owe you anything – certainly not a delay in rolling up my first case in a way that's going to help my career.'

'I could make you.'

'How?'

'You wouldn't thank me if you found out.'

'Now you're just bluffing. I call.' She turned to face me, locking those deep-blue eyes of hers on mine. It was obvious that her looks had got in the way of her being treated seriously back at Thames House, equally obvious that she resented the hell out of the fact, and even more obvious that she wasn't going to take anything less than a direct order from the Queen as an indication that she should give way. I couldn't help liking that about her: for all her charms she was made of steel underneath. That made what I was about to do feel cheap, since I would have preferred to make a willing ally out of her.

'Dammit, Penny, why do we have to fight like this? We've got the same goal; I just have more data than you about what's going on.'

'Of course you do. I've been inside for a year, working through the hierarchy. I've built a reputation with them, got inside their command structure and earned their trust. Now all of a sudden you swan in, right into the High Council no less, and think you're going to start giving orders? You've been here five bloody minutes and think you know everything. Well, I've got news for you, sunshine: you don't. You don't know which departments are compromised, who's got pawns where or where the money is. I do. I even ran your background check, for Christ's sake. So don't get on your high horse and start waving your dick about just because you think you can – try fitting in with what's already in place and help me take these bastards down.' She was maintaining a calm exterior as she said all this, but her eyes were full of fury. Anyone watching from a distance wouldn't know that she was tearing a strip off me, even as I kept my face in a comfortable smile. From a distance, we were still a couple trying to see if we fitted together.

'No, Penny, there's more. What you know is going to help, but it won't stop what they're doing. I don't know exactly what the plan is yet, but I need to find out before we can roll them up. That way we can make sure it only has to happen once. If any of them get away to talk about it, there's the chance that they'll just find a different route.'

'But they've already got their fingers all over the place. They must have influence over a good half of the economy. What more do they want?'

'They're planning to take over.'

'Yeah, right. They might have money, but they don't have the forces to seize power.'

'Like I said, I don't know everything yet. But if they find another way to achieve their objective, anything you do to shut them down now will end up being useless. We only get one shot, and it needs to be perfect.'

'So you're going to kill them all.'

'I hope not, but I can't form a plan without data. If you try to shut them down now I won't be able to get that.'

'I'll need to report in.'

'Don't mention me.'

'I have to. I'm willing to play along with you, but I need to explain why.'

'Your people aren't cleared for that.'

'What's that supposed to mean?'

'That they mustn't know I'm here. Your lot aren't authorised to know about what my lot are up to. Surely the amount of trouble you had finding me must have been a clue?'

'Not the point. I have to report what happens here, and when someone I think to be an Army Intelligence officer tells me to back off, that needs to be reported.' Damn, just as I thought I wouldn't have to do it.

'I can give you a very good reason, but you won't like it. Take me on trust.'

'No.'

'Please?' That came out without thought. Something was holding me back from using the key that would give me every-thing I wanted. Morals? Manners? I wasn't sure.

'I can't, and that's it. I'll cooperate for now, but your presence here has to go in my report.'

'Arse.'

'For what it's worth, I'm sorry. But I have to follow orders.'

'I know, Penny. That makes this all the more difficult.' She instantly stiffened, expecting me to hit her. She opened the space between us a little, making room to defend herself. It was a good prep move, and might have done her some good if hitting her was what I had in mind. Field training seemed to have agreed with her. I stood still as she watched me carefully.

'Makes what all the harder?' No choice, then.

'In Westminster Abbey, a thousand years ago, there was a statue.' Penny's eyes started to widen.

'Oh, you have *got* to be fucking kidding me.'

'The statue,' I continued, 'was of a man named Balthazar. Seven feet high, it stood upon the space reserved for the altar as the church went up around it. Balthazar's arms were spread wide as a benediction upon the builders, who thought he was a saint. He was not, and once the church had been completed the statue was reduced to rubble – a sacrifice to bless the holy place.'

'Crap.'

'You are familiar with the story?'

'Yes.'

'Good.' The story, which was complete nonsense, served as a

recognition phrase keyed specifically to her for this one operation. By reciting it, I'd just told Miss Marsh that I was from an agency that outranked hers and that she now worked for me. I'd also made myself feel like shit for pulling rank on her. I'd have to report using it, since it had just completely destroyed my cover as far as she was concerned. 'For what it's worth, Penny, I'm sorry.'

'Are you really?' She didn't sound convinced. 'I suppose this explains all the manipulation, the blackmail, the cajoling. It must have been much more fun to do that than be honest.'

'That's not—'

'Spare me. So now I just do as I'm told, do I? Without a clue as to who I'm working for? Just as I was about to get things cleaned up nicely and start making a difference, you come along and screw things up.'

'Not necessarily.'

'Oh, really?'

'Yeah, really. Keep on doing what you've been doing so far, and we'll coordinate our efforts. If we play this right, you'll still get the credit and everyone gets what they deserve.'

'Fine.' It didn't sound fine, but that's women for you.

'Oh, and I think we should start dating.'

'What?' That didn't sound fine, either.

'It gives us a reason to talk. Since we've already got them convinced that we're interested in each other, albeit for different reasons than they think, let's play along with that and keep them comfy.'

'I'm not having sex with you.'

'Good.'

'What?' She seemed affronted that I wouldn't want to.

'Sex would make it messy. We might end up staying at each other's places, but this is purely business.' Not that I would have objected under other circumstances – she was as stunning as ever and I'd quite fancied the idea of taking a tumble with her for a long while, but I wasn't going to let this be anything other than strictly business.

'Oh. Right.'

'We should go back. Who's this photographer you've got watching the house?'

'A freelancer. He thinks he's working for the papers.'

'Not Service?'

'Oh, good God, no.'

'That's something.'

Back at the house, I wasted no time in finding Folkestone. He was in the middle of drilling a group of foot soldiers, the men who'd be guarding the ritual due to take place the following night. He didn't look overly happy to be interrupted, but saluted crisply and came to hear what I had to say.

'I was just out for a walk and saw something unusual. Have we got long-range sentries watching the grounds?'

'Some, why?'

'Because either they were trying to peep in on what I was up to in the gardens or we've got someone else out there. Either way, they're not doing their job.'

'Show me.' We found a plan of the grounds and I indicated a reasonable place for a theoretical watcher to be. Folkestone looked curious. 'I'll check it out, sir.' The deference was new, and presumably a sign of his growing respect for me. It was an interesting detail on the side for now, though, since I needed that photographer gone before he could deliver my picture to the outside world. It was also a useful way to show Folkestone that I was on side, since the usual Intelligence Services wouldn't dream of offering up one of their own as a tactical sacrifice. The odds were that he'd get beaten up a bit, forced to spill his guts and then taken out for a nine-millimetre sleeping pill – an unfortunate situation, but necessary as far as I was concerned.

Chapter Thirteen

By the time I joined the interrogation, Folkestone had already been working on the poor bastard all night. It was the smell that hit me first – a combination of faeces, burned flesh and chemicals, with a side order of disinfectant – and despite the best efforts of a sizeable extractor fan the room was heavy with it. Folkestone himself was standing in the corner when I entered, his face shiny with sweat as he looked over his instruments as though deciding what he was going to do next. I managed to watch the process he went through impassively – my actions had brought the poor bastard there and I deserved to face the consequences.

So I had to stand there without reacting. That was a lot easier for me than it was for the photographer. My real problem came afterwards.

It wasn't the first time I'd had tea with a torturer, but Folkestone wasn't the professional type I'm used to. This was pure sociopath, a man who took joy from his art and wanted to share it. I listened as Folkestone talked, detailing what he'd done already, how he'd worked out the techniques from horror movies, concentration camp footage and reports from human rights charities. That last group made him laugh, since he was willing to bet that their lurid descriptions of abuses in the Third World weren't meant to be taken as creative tips. He'd married all this to his training as a paramedic and was proud of the result, since there were only so many old ladies and drunks he could quietly 'prune' in the back of a moving ambulance before people started getting suspicious. Once he'd been spotted and recruited by the Eagle Society, he'd had the chance to really develop his talents with the kind of facilities he'd always wanted. No more deserted warehouses for him, and no more trouble trying to kidnap homeless people on his own. The Society had been able to help him find a supply of subjects for his experiments and the discreet way in which they did it meant he'd be able to carry on for as long as he wanted. It wasn't as if the subjects mattered anyway, since they were nobodies to Folkestone, the kind of people no one would miss and all the nice folks wanted rid of anyway. His work was helping to remove the detritus of society at the same time as advancing his art.

He was, of course, writing a book about it all, and thought that it had a good chance of becoming a classic. Given some of the rubbish they publish these days, I wouldn't have been surprised if it did.

All the time we were taking our tea, the look of horror on the photographer's face as Folkestone prepared his instruments for each new phase came back to me in flashes. All those references to concentration camp 'experiments' made sense in light of what I'd just witnessed, but there was an element of imagination there that just compounded the evil of the whole thing. Folkestone had talked me through what he was doing, too, showing off his education and his skills as though he wanted to impress me. More of the deference thing, I suppose, and after what I'd done to Flory he must have thought I'd be impressed by his own work. Quite the opposite – I do what I have to because I have to do it. I'm not proud of the things I've done for Queen and Country, and showing off the way Folkestone had was anathema to me. Underneath the poker face of my cover, I was appalled. Appalled at what I'd seen, appalled at the existence of men who do this kind of thing and take pleasure from it, and appalled at myself not just for providing the victim but for being able to stand there and watch as all those things took place less than ten feet away from me. I can honestly say that I've never been so grateful to see a man die as I was that morning in the cellars of Austen Hall.

I ate lunch with Miss Marsh, picking at my food while I suppressed the memories and she talked about what the women were doing to prepare for that night. It was finally time for the ritual and the place was buzzing. Torches had been put in place, altar cloths cleaned and pressed, the site cleared of debris and decorated with flags and flowers. It sounded like a regular country fayre, all very traditional and thoroughly wholesome. The troops had been drilling in the gardens outside while the women worked, and a couple were the subject of some discussion, as apparently was Miss Marsh's good fortune in bagging me. According to gossip, Michael and I were the only unmarried members of the Council and, even if I was only an associate member, I was ahead of him in the fanciable stakes. His money didn't seem to cut much ice with the women, and apparently he'd tried it on with most of them at one time or another and had managed to leave a bad impression every time. Quiet confidence and good manners were the way to their hearts, and Penny was kind enough to give them confirmation of my ample supply of both.

I wasn't able to tell her anything of that morning's events, nor of any contingency plans for the evening, since we already had tasks assigned to us that would fill the rest of the day – Penny was to finish preparing the site and I was expected to rest, meditate and be ready for the ritual at seven. We parted company with a kiss on the cheek, much to the approval of several lady witnesses.

*

As the summer evening started to cool, I joined the twelve other members of the circle outside the main entrance. A quartet of Range Rovers was waiting for us, identically silver and shining as if they'd just left the showroom. We settled ourselves in and set out for the ritual site, each of us in crisp black uniforms like staff officers on the way to a meeting – which I suppose we were in a way. The site was about half an hour's drive away, still in the grounds but far from the eyes of anyone we couldn't trust or the likely routes of ramblers. Given the sort of treatment Folkestone would delight in handing out to trespassers, this struck me as a good idea for more than just the usual reason. We were delivered to a clearing on the edge of some woods, where final preparations were made, ties straightened and a few last minutes spent waiting for the correct moment to begin. Finally someone looked at the sky, checked their watch and gave the nod. It was time.

I saw the torches first, a trooper on each side of the path lighting them as they walked towards us to form an avenue of fire marking our route to the ritual site. Their boots crunched on the path as they marched sternly, faces set like stone, until they finally reached us and raised their right arms in silent salute. We nodded to them, acknowledging their work, then started our walk. Drums began to beat from out of sight, marking time for us as we approached. The forest was otherwise silent, a sign that the animals had quite sensibly decided to bugger off and leave us to it – and I couldn't blame them.

It must have taken ten minutes to walk the path, lit all the way by a torch every dozen paces or so. The drums were spaced every five torches, so I knew where most of Folkestone's man-power was for this part of the ritual. It was a bloody good set-up, too. Making a decent entrance can be a major help in ritual and this was one for the history books. The uniforms, the drums, the grim purpose in our footsteps – all combined to give a real feeling of power building in ourselves and a sense of grand importance, the sense of being at the very centre of things among men who could move the universe by sheer force of will alone.

Eventually, the path widened and we came to the place that had been prepared. A ring of torches marked the edges of the clearing, with a banner at each quarter hanging from a polished brass standard topped with an eagle. A different rune was marked on each one – the elements associated with each banner's position. In the north was the altar, draped with black cloth edged in gold and marked with a curved swastika. This was the first time I'd seen the group use one, and its shape was straight from the occult societies behind the Nazi Party in its early days. If I needed a sign that this was more than just politics with added window dressing, I had it now. This was the real deal – the Sun Whisk – the force of creation reversed and held sacred by the nastiest ends of the Nazi cult. This proved all the concerns right, and confirmed that I was in the right place. We were well out of MI5 and Miss Marsh's jurisdiction, and slap bang in the middle of mine.

As we moved to our appointed places, the chanting began. Each of us had a slightly different mantra to recite, and the effect seemed to harmonise in a weird way that really shouldn't have worked musically. If you'd taken one part out, the whole thing would have fallen apart, but between us we had a bloody powerful energy build-up on the go. It was already starting to get colder, and the shadows outside the circle were lengthening faster than they had any right to. Time and space were beginning to bend around us, moulding in line with our collective will.

This was some serious magic.

Gold was standing in the middle by the altar, his hands raised high as his part of the chant slid into guttural words and harsh sounds. The look in his eyes was ecstatic, like a shaman at full tilt, his face rapt like a whirling dervish. I couldn't quite make out what he was saying, but it didn't sound all that friendly.

A mist drifted across the ground, held within the circle of torches but filling it to lap around our ankles. Damn, but it was cold. Cold enough to leech the heat from my body and make me feel like ice from the knees down. It rose as we chanted, our rhythm steady, until it was up as far as our waists. I could see patterns forming in the swirls – faces screaming, hands reaching out towards me, a hint of something bigger and far nastier than human moving sinuously between them. The currents became more pronounced and what had been impressions became more coherent. I felt something brush my leg, unseen fingertips grabbing desperately at my trousers without success. Then the shapes were gone, and in their place was a definite current, more controlled, focused, directed. The mist circled inside the torches, an eye in the centre like a storm, and became more concentrated as it swirled faster and faster. As the speed increased, the pattern became tighter and the mist moved away from the torches and towards the centre. Still we chanted, on and on as though nothing were happening.

The mist quickly became a column in the centre of our circle. A wall of white that spun like a tornado. I could hear it now, the sound of countless voices in agony and terror, and there was a distinct edge of sulphur in the air. The torches were burning brightly – too brightly – each one crowned with a pillar of fire five feet high and blood red. And yet above the chanting and the screaming I could hear Gold's voice as he shouted towards the mist.

'. . . ler! Come forward! Step beyond your prison and return to us!'

Oh. Shit.

'Reveal yourself! The way is open!'

The shape of a hand became visible behind that wall of white, pressing against it from the inside. A bulge started to show around it, and details became more distinct. I could see the individual fingers, the shape of its palm leading down towards the wrist. It pressed further, the beginnings of an arm coming into view as the hand broke free of the wall holding it in. There was a face above it, just the chin and nose, but enough to get an impression. Now I could see his jaw, his open mouth and, above the mouth, the shape of a moustache . . .

Suddenly the red flames around us turned a bright and shining white. The pillar of mist became one of flame, white to match the torches. The swirling pillar of fire grew, like a sudden hurricane that filled the circle for a horrible second that lasted for ever. I was having trouble staying on my feet, but the mantra seemed to be protecting me, just barely, and I focused on controlling the panic rising inside me enough to keep chanting. A roaring filled my ears, blotting out the sound of my own voice, an inferno mixed with screams that made my blood run cold in spite of the heat that was already making my clothes smoulder. Then, as suddenly as it had begun, it was over. The torches, the banners, even the altar itself were reduced to ashes where they had stood. People around me fell to their knees, vomiting loudly. One figure on the other side of the circle seemed to be having a heart attack; another was catatonic – lying on the ground in a foetal position. I sympathised.

I've walked in the lands of the dead. I've seen gods made flesh and demons push through the walls of reality to feast on the flesh of the living. But that was the closest I'd ever been to Hell.

We gathered up our wounded, tended where we could and dragged ourselves back down the path toward the cars. That path, which had seemed like a triumphal procession on the way in, felt more like the road out of Russia on the way home.

Chapter Fourteen

We took stock back at the house. There was no point trying to disguise the identity of who we'd been trying to reach, but while we talked about what had gone wrong, the name wasn't mentioned at all. Folkestone's paramedic training had come in handy for making sure that the heart attack hadn't been fatal, but one of our number was still curled up in a corner of the room, rocking back and forth on his heels while he sang nursery rhymes to himself, in exactly the same spot where we'd left him half an hour previously. That was going to take a bit of explaining, given that he was supposed to be in a meeting with the Bank of England three days later. I was quite sure that would be taken care of, though, since Mr Green turned out to be fairly high up in the Treasury and would be able to excuse the absence. In the meantime, our little rocking ball of wibble would be off to a nice place in the country for a bit of a lie down.

But the question remained: what had gone wrong?

That was pretty simple, to be honest, and had two driving factors behind it. For a start, we were trying to break someone out of Hell. Not the metaphor, not an alternative dimension or the plains of purgatory where the dead roam around and I've been known to take the occasional stroll, but the one you heard about in Sunday School. It's had any number of names over the years, depending on who, when and where you are at the time, but it's still the same maximum-security afterlife where the really bad people go. Punishment central. Eternal damnation, torture and all that good stuff. The kind of place where serial killers, mad dictators and A & R men go. It's not the kind of place that's designed to let you out easily, and the staff are *very* touchy about people from this side of the fence trying to tunnel through. We were pretty lucky to be alive, all in all.

The other factor was me, in a way. Or at least the Service. When I was an innocent trainee bastard, between recruitment and deployment, part of the training was a brief history of the people I work for. The Service came into being as it is now during the last war, the job previously having been taken care of by gentlemen adventurers who were willing to do the nasty on an ad hoc basis as they came across bad people who needed a bit of a spanking. With the Nazis, however, the need for something more focused became apparent and so the Service was born as a mix of occultists and commandos who could take the fight to old Adolf on the same fields he and his cronies were so keen on. All over the world, as Hitler's minions searched for the Spear of Destiny, the Skull of Death, the Fountain of Eternal Youth and suchlike, people like me were popping up and getting in the way. One of the most famous from back then was a man named Vincent Alexander, the man who finally got close enough to kill Hitler and end the war in 1953. The big fighting might have been over for eight years by then, but Hitler had managed to escape to South America and was hiding out with a plan to start over when the time was right. Vincent, a failed actor who had a weird kind of charisma that just persuaded people to do whatever he wanted, strolled past the guards, into the house, right into Hitler's study and apparently gave a twenty-minute report that bored everyone in the room senseless before pulling out his pistol and shooting the Führer five times in the head. He then went to work on everyone else with, according to the story, a straight razor and the kind of focus a true psychopath can bring to a fight when his life's on the line. By the time the guards actually got in Vincent was alone, and managed to convince them that he'd killed the attacker – a completely loyal man who'd been with them since they left Germany. He returned home to a medal, a retirement and a quietly arranged suicide: it seemed that Vincent had developed a taste for killing people in his off-duty time as well, and with his usefulness over there was no way he'd be allowed back into polite society.

The story was told to us partly as a history, and partly as a warning about what happens when you start to like your work. I figure I'm reasonably safe from that: killing's my job, and I don't see it becoming my hobby any time soon.

But the point is that *we* killed Hitler. And we were thorough about it, too: specially enchanted bullets in the gun and a bunch of magicians making sure he went exactly where he was supposed to without any chance for someone to get clever about inter-cepting his soul en route. We still have people doing that now, keeping an eye on him and a couple of others we don't want back to be sure that nobody manages to pull off what the Eagle Society had been trying to do. Those guys had almost certainly been involved in things going wrong during the ritual, spiking our energy pattern with a carefully circumspect counter-pattern of their own to make sure that Hell's own defences saw exactly what we were up to. I made a mental note to send them a bottle of something – if I hadn't known they were out there I would have written the whole thing off as an accident.

Fortunately for the good guys, the men of the Eagle Society (with my help) came to the conclusion that we hadn't had enough strength to get through rather than thinking of enemy action as a likely possibility. New ideas were mooted, and when the final verdict was in we were to change tack a little. Obviously we weren't going to be able to warn our target of his upcoming extraction, but the mechanisms were to be prepared for an

attempt later in the year. It was also time, apparently, to move
into Phase Two of preparations – something I figured I'd be
hearing more about later.

After a much-needed night's sleep and a very late breakfast, I
embarked on a Phase Two of my own: Miss Marsh.

'What the fuck was that last night?' She was rattled, and clearly
out of her comfort zone. I'd been told not to give her details,
and that worked fine for me.

'Special effects gone wrong.'

'What?'

'Right. You've seen *Triumph of the Will*, yes? All the marching,
torches, searchlights and stuff?'

'Ye-es. What's that got to do with this?'

'Same thing. All that malarkey last night was supposed to be
a show for the troops. Evidence of divine providence being on
our side, and so on. Something to give you lot a bit more steel
in your backbones. The thought is that some of the pyrotechnics
must have short-circuited and set everything off out of sequence,
which is why it all went pear-shaped.'

'And the chanting? You were in there, so you must know what
that was about.'

'More showbiz. This lot are big on their occult imagery, so it
was a natural choice to make the show a big black magic thing.
It didn't actually mean anything.'

'How come you know so much about it?'

'Background training. How did you get your politics right?'

'Oh.'

'Same thing.'

'I'm not sure that I believe you.'

'Your choice. We have to trust each other here: I'm relying on
you not to turn me in, either to these shits or your bosses back
at Thames House, and you need to believe that I'm not going to

lie to you about what's going on in places you can't get to. Between us we can put the best picture together and act properly when the time comes.'

'I don't exactly have much choice about that, do I?'

'I didn't want to say it quite like that, but now you mention it, no. How are the troops?'

'Confused. We've not been told much about last night – before or after – so there are rumours flying around like crazy. One man tried telling me earlier that you lot were going to bring Hitler back from the dead, for crying out loud. I think there's a good chance here to cause some real damage to their morale if we play it right. I just need to plant another crazy rumour or two and be careful not to make too much fuss while I do it.'

'No.'

'Why not?'

'Because if Folkestone goes through the rumours and tracks them down to sources you'll be in a lot of trouble.'

'Then protect me – hold him off.'

'Not a chance. That might swing suspicion my way, which is exactly what would happen if you came up as a rumour source. Keep your head down and act like a true believer, a faithful follower. If we play this right there's a good chance we can use it to move closer to what's really going on.'

'Which is what?'

'I'm not sure yet, but it's bigger than I thought. Given the people we can see, it's a sure thing that there are people we can't who are even bigger. If we're going to take this lot out properly then we need the head, not just the body. Shut this down and they'll wait, re-form and quietly build another group – which we'd have to find and take out again. I want to do this just the once, and I don't think either of us are particularly keen on another year or two undercover putting up with this kind of crap, are we? I wouldn't mind having a life, given half a chance.'

'A life?'

'Yeah, a life. You got a problem with the idea?'

'You just don't strike me as the kind of person who has a life outside. You're all about the job; no time for relationships, friends or anything else. Able to drop everything and disappear for as long as you have to. You wouldn't be here if you weren't.'

'Much like you, then.'

'Yeah.' She seemed sad at that. 'Just like me. But at least I've got opportunities, and I think you've been doing this so long that you don't know how to be anything else.'

'So you don't think I could give this up and settle down?'

'What would you do? I don't think they've got a section for infiltration and assassination down at the Job Centre. At least I've got the rest of the Civil Service to choose from, but if you're as secret as you're letting me believe then you haven't got a hope.'

'Shows how much you know. There's more to me than you think.'

'Oh, I'm quite sure of that, I'm just not convinced it's stuff that works in the real world. But then I'm not likely to find out, am I? You'll finish this assignment and disappear behind another false name and a new cover as you head off to save the world again.'

'Actually, I was planning on a holiday.'

'Who as?' She had me there. I was still trying to work out how the conversation had turned personal and things were becoming profoundly uncomfortable. I wasn't there to explain myself to Miss Marsh, I was there to get any information she may have had, to make sure she didn't screw things up for me and to continue establishing our identity as a cover for when we got back to London. The arm I had around her waist was simply an extension of the act for anyone who might happen to see us, as was the arm she had around mine.

'Back to business.'

'But of course. Doesn't do to let people see your human side, does it?'

'Not while we're working, no. I don't fancy being killed over a discussion of what I'm going to do when the war's over, and I've seen enough films to know what happens to the guy who'll be getting married when that one last mission is over. Eyes on the job, Penny, and we'll turn back into humans when we're finished.'

'I'll believe that when I see it. Any other orders, sir?'

'No, just keep your head down for now and we'll wait for the dust to settle before deciding our next move.'

'As you wish.' There was a glint in her eye – she'd won the point, and she knew it.

We moved out of the gardens and back towards the house. To be honest, I was glad the conversation was over – Miss Marsh had managed to run rings around me there in a way I didn't like at all, and I was starting to wonder what might happen if I let her get under my skin like that again.

Our catatonic banker needed to be transferred, and I watched Folkestone showing an entirely different side of his character as he slowly manoeuvred his patient to the car. It wasn't that the man couldn't move, just that he'd return to the foetal position every time he was left alone. Under Folkestone's gentle care he walked down the steps, regarding each one with a questioning expression and carefully moving his weight as though he thought they might give out under him at any moment. I didn't exactly have much in the way of sympathy for him, really: he'd deliberately chosen to help open a gateway to Hell. I might not have known that was the plan, but everyone else seemed to and that pissed me off as well. In fact, that was something I might be able to use. The car carrying our colleague slipped down the driveway in a rustle of gravel, and another car pulled out behind it carrying an old man whose heart needed a good looking at.

This effectively left us two men down at worst, one if the doctors cleared Henry Johnon's ticker. Johnon was a solicitor with more influential clients than anyone wanted to think about: the entire membership of the Eagle Society had either him or one of his partners on permanent retainer, and there was a mutual fixing deal that took care of any small issues that might otherwise inconvenience their business interests. It turned out that Folkestone's official day job was as his 'assistant', for which we read 'fixer' – someone who wouldn't be afraid to use blackmail, bribery, coercion or violence to secure his employer's interests and those of his clients.

Even with Johnon we'd still have to find a new body to fill the space left by our banker, and there was also the matter of the funds he handled on the Society's behalf. Apparently that was going to be my job, at least in the short term, although I argued just enough that my position in the bank wasn't sufficiently senior to get away with it. I was to relax and do as I was told, and more suitable arrangements would be made while I held the fort. I couldn't have planned it better – even if it was just for a couple of days, I was going to hold the purse-strings. Plenty of time for me to map out where their money was and pass the information back to the Boss, so we could bankrupt them later. To be honest, it was more likely to end up in our own budget: tempting though the idea was, I doubted we'd be allowed to get away with screwing the economy just so we could fuck with a few dozen people we were about to kill. Especially not after that mess we had with the stock market last time somebody tried it. Apparently global recessions are so much against government policy that even we have to pay attention.

All that remained after that was clearing up the site. I think we'd all been looking for other things to do as a way of putting this off, but there was no way we could leave it in its current state. We'd abandoned it as it was the previous evening, with the remains of the torches and everything else just lying there for any idiot to find. Bad form, that, and that's without considering what it was going to be like on a psychic level.

We got our first taste of that last detail as we approached the site. There was a chill in the air that didn't fit with the warm evening, and the clean-up crew was not looking happy. They told us that they had managed most of the torches but the last hundred yards was too cold for them to enter. That and something in the air was unsettling them, making them constantly look over their shoulders and reach for weapons they weren't carrying. Just as well they weren't – judging by how jumpy they were we'd have had a nasty accident by now. We sent them back to their vehicles with strict instructions to tell no one about what they'd seen or felt. We were going to take care of the problem and make sure that they could finish the job they'd been given.

The path leading towards the ritual site was still pretty impressive even in daylight. The twilight, torches and drums had really done a number, of course, but the raw material was pretty damned good to start with. It was getting chillier around us as we walked, and by the time we reached the torches it was cold enough to make our breath mist in clouds around us. We were definitely right to have checked on this ourselves.

I was left to guard the entrance, much to my annoyance. I wanted to get a look at what they were planning to do about this – it was just too good an opportunity for me to see how clever they really were. But orders are orders, and the lecture I'd given Penny only a few hours earlier was still ringing in my ears. I knew that a certain amount of it was bullshit for her benefit, but the legendary low-profile approach was more likely to serve me best at this point.

One of the others came around the corner and into range, still within the path of torches, and beckoned me in. It seemed a little odd at first, but it was the chance I wanted to give them a closer eyeball. Up the path, around the corner and into the circle itself . . .

Into blackness.

Ahead of me I could see something big, scaly, angry-looking and obviously demonic in nature – the harsh stink of brimstone was a pretty good clue there. Its tail was twitching as it turned its head to regard us, then stilled momentarily before its body followed, ready to spring. One of Hitler's warders, at a guess, sent to let us know how unhappy his boss was about our interference. This was one of those moments when I could see strong advantages to letting him eat the lot of us – it would take the group out quite effectively, that was for sure, and if it meant me dying there as well then so be it. However, there was that niggling matter of Phase Two to worry about, and anyone else who might be in on the plot, and the very clear fact that a short cut to Hell didn't appeal in the slightest. I was going to have to help these bastards avoid their just desserts, albeit temporarily, and save their lives. The decision clicked into place as I was leaping for cover – the demon was getting its groove on.

Who says the universe doesn't have a sense of humour?

Chapter Fifteen

There are a few basic principles to being stuck in a fight with a demon in an alternative dimension, and as luck would have it this was the sort of thing that was covered in my basic training. Horses for courses – some people learn to handle a bayonet, some learn how to steer a ship and a few lucky bastards get to learn the best way of kicking a demon's head in. Judging by the carnage that my scaly friend was wreaking, I was the only one here who'd taken that particular course.

The first thing you do is try to understand the rules. Everywhere has them, even if they vary wildly from place to place, and if you're going to fight you need to work out how. The demon before me didn't ring any bells from the *Goetia* so it was either wearing a different face or was a low-level functionary sent as a matter of form. Since there was no reason for it to be the former, my guess was that it was the demonic equivalent of a minor civil servant. That was good, since it wouldn't be packing the kind of power you'd experience with a full-on Demon Prince of Hell – a sight most people only ever get to see once. In essence, then, what I had to deal with was a brawler.

The next question is how do the rules apply to me? The only way to work that out is experimentation. It's very tempting to just charge straight in and engage the enemy, but that's an easy way to get your arse handed to you on a plate. Calm, level-headed care is what gets you through moments like this and your opponent is going to want to bollocks that up. You'll want to do the same thing to him in due course, which is what makes charging in seem like such an attractive option, but one step at a time. Start by drawing power, finding out what you've got to call on once the fight begins. A slow breath to centre yourself, and then gently start to pull energy in.

I was a lucky man on this occasion: the power I was absorbing was way beyond what I can manage in the normal world. I decided to reach inside myself for a weapon, just to see what happened; no gun, which wasn't a surprise really since I've never thought of myself as a pistolero, but something else presented itself to me and I was only too happy to wrap my fingers around it and bring my hand out for a look.

It was my dear old friend, the Fairbairn-Sykes knife.

Guns are noisy and make you lazy. Tossers like big shiny things they saw in a movie once and Bruce Lee wannabes will pick any one of a wide selection of converted farm implements that seemed like a much better idea three hundred years ago on an island where weaponry was banned. I suppose I could have gone for a flaming sword if I fancied the matching armour, but what I got was exactly what I wanted – this little piece of metal has been my preferred instrument of antisocial behaviour for my entire adult life and I saw no reason to change it just because I was fighting something with about eight times my body mass. The demon was a brawler and, with the right knife in my hand, I'm a fucking surgeon.

And it was time to prove that point. The demon had its claws wrapped around some poor sod's head, ready to shake it until something came loose, so I slipped in behind it and let the knife trace a path straight through its ... well, if it had been human I'd have said Achilles tendon. Whatever you want to call it, the demon sure as hell noticed. He dropped his rag doll, turned to face me and roared straight in my face. It needed a mint.

It might have been expecting me to go rigid with terror, or be overwhelmed by the noise, smell and sight of its teeth, but I'm willing to bet that the one thing it wasn't expecting was a knife in the goolies. I'm a London boy, and if you think noise, bad smells and a load of front are going to bother me then you're in for a major disappointment. I pulled the knife out as the beast screamed in pain and reversed my grip as I stepped out and turned around to its rear, giving me the perfect opportunity to stab the back of its kneecap. That put both legs in the 'damaged' file, which would hamper its movement, and its knackers in the 'ouch' category, which was probably going to have an adverse effect on its peace of mind.

Looking around as I moved, I couldn't see any sign of edges to the area, nor of anyone else around me. Whoever the demon had been using as a chew toy seemed to have evaporated away, and the fight was a straight one-on-one. Whether this meant that everyone else had already been killed or we were in individual fights, I couldn't tell, so the only thing left to do was get my own backside out of trouble as quickly as possible. The demon was limping, which was good, and looking like it wanted to use me as toilet paper for the next infinity or so, which was an awful lot better than you'd think. Angry people, or demons, or Great Old Ones or whatever, fuck up. Anger clouds judgement and can lead to impetuous actions that end badly. Like the charge that the demon was launching at me, for example. It was easy enough to dive and roll clear, then come up with a kick to the back of the knee I'd just used as a temporary home for my knife. The knee might have been at waist height on me, but a solid, straight side-kick put enough extra bend in it to cause a good stagger.

The demon turned to face me again, and I found myself wishing for a red cloak: there are enough bulls out there known as 'El Diablo' for the imagery to be worth a bit of a giggle.

Laughing at the thing made it even angrier – it was used to people screaming, running away in terror and all that performance, so having a bloke stand there laughing must have been bad for its self-esteem or something.

Another charge, and this time I stepped just far enough clear to avoid it. A dash up the back, a good leap and I was perched between its shoulders with an arm reaching around its throat. The idea of choking the bastard out was appealing, but efficiency was in charge now. The knife went in hard, right where the I-guess-you-could-call-it-a-spine met the skull. My opponent went down like a puppet with its strings cut, and as we hit the deck together I found myself kneeling in the clearing. Just like that: one moment in another dimension, the next back in the real world.

Around the circle, I could see the others. Most were starting to move, but it looked as though a couple of them had passed out. Acting on instinct, I started checking pulses, but the first immobile figure took me aback. The look on his face was one of unspeakable terror, that of a man scared straight to death. I couldn't help wondering what the demon had done to get that kind of reaction, and whether this was the figure I'd seen the demon playing with when I arrived. Whatever had happened to him, there was no point wasting time now. We'd lost three in all – each wearing that same look: one High Court judge, a high-end company director on about a dozen different boards and a Permanent Undersecretary at the Ministry of Defence. Three more plausible excuses to be constructed and delivered to their families and friends. Three less people for me to worry about, too, and a chance that from this I could move into a position with better access to what was happening behind the scenes. There was no way I could have got away with this kind of pruning, so Hell's minion had done me a major favour.

We arranged transporting the bodies ourselves. The

atmosphere that had scared the workers so thoroughly before our arrival was gone now, so they were put to work again covering up the evidence of our passing. The return journey to the house was silent, as each man considered his experiences, and that silence didn't break until we were assembled around a bottle of single malt behind closed and locked doors. Only then did people feel able to start speaking of what had happened.

Their stories shared a common pattern, beginning with a sudden change to darkness from the world around them. Each had then faced the same creature I had seen, with varying responses. Many had tried to flee; some had sought weapons around them; but none had thought of hiding. Perhaps that was the mistake the casualties had made. We had only seen each other when the demon was in contact with us, so the likelihood was that we had indeed all faced the same foe. I was the only one, it appeared, who thought of finding a weapon within myself, and I was certainly the only one who'd taken the fight to the demon rather than trying to escape it. Mr White, who I now knew to be something on the General Staff, seemed particularly impressed by this, and a little annoyed with himself for not thinking of it as well.

'Well done, John,' he said. 'This shows exactly what's wrong with the Army – all the smart people like you are leaving. Those bloody idiots in Whitehall are happy enough to make their own jobs cushier, but while the troops are being treated badly enough to want to leave, there's no future in it for any of us. Better to stay at home and sort things out here first than piss around as America's trained poodle.' I didn't have to act much to agree with him on that one, since I've known quite a few soldiers over the years and what's happened to them over the last decade has been disgusting.

'Looks like you saved us all, John,' said someone behind me.

There were murmurs of general assent. The irony that I was planning to kill every other person in the room wasn't lost on me, since the general assent looked to be smack on the money. Just to add to the thing, my response was completely accurate from whichever identity I looked at it:

'Just doing my duty.'

There was a knock at the door.

'Come.'

I don't know who I was expecting, but it wasn't Miss Marsh. Her eyes quickly took in the assembled company, undoubtedly noticing that we were now three more men short.

'Message, sir. The cars carrying Mr Johnon and Mr Ffoulkes crashed about an hour ago. Mr Johnon and his driver were killed.'

'Both crashed?' asked Gold.

'Yes, sir. At about the same time, as far as we can tell.'

'Thank you, Miss Gentle. You may go.' Penny flashed me a look that spoke volumes about wanting to be let in on the game, and left.

'So that leaves us five men down.' The statement was an obvious one, but White seemed to deem it worth saying. 'Think the crashes are related to our little adventure?'

'I would have thought that was obvious!' Gold's mood was going rapidly downhill. 'We can work with nine, but some changes will have to be made to the basic plan. Mr Dennis, there will be work for you in addition to the other tasks you're taking on. Will you be able to manage?'

'I'll do my best, sir.' Well, what else do you say?

'Good. Phase Two will still be going ahead, while Mr Dennis and Folkestone work to redress the balance in another direction. Keep an eye on Folkestone, by the way: he can get a little . . . enthusiastic sometimes.'

*

'You seem a bit preoccupied.' Miss Marsh made a fine job of stating the obvious. 'What happened this afternoon? Where are Compton, Webb and Granger?'

'Dead.'

'Dead?'

'Dead. Don't ask how, because I can't tell you. But it wasn't me. In fact, there'd be more corpses to cover up if I hadn't been there.'

'You expect me to accept that?'

'Need to know, Penny. There are certain things that, if I told you, could put your life in danger – and not just from these people.' I was understating things a little, to be honest. There were certain things I could tell her that would leave her locked up in Broadmoor or dead in a ditch, courtesy of my friends back in the Service. Somehow I wasn't all that sure she'd take an account of my afternoon seriously, anyway.

'Your mysterious masters?'

'My mysterious masters. They prefer to remain mysterious, and aren't afraid of making sure they do.'

'Bullshit. That never happens in real life. The Intelligence Services don't run around killing people – it causes too much fuss. You'll be telling me that MI5 kills people next.'

I mentioned the name of a recently deceased government official, and she shut up.

'We need to sort out dating when we get back. Shall I take you out later in the week?'

'Take me ... Oh, yes.' Penny's thoughts were obviously still running with the chances of being killed by her own side. 'Somewhere nice, too. Try to impress me.'

'If I really wanted to do that, I'd cook you something.' That got me a look.

'You cook? I wouldn't have thought you were the type.'

'You'd be surprised.' There was no way I'd ever tell her that in my outside job I had actually played guitar on some of the CDs in her own collection. She seemed to have decided that I had no private life, that there was nothing between missions. Maybe she thought I lived in a capsule, pulled out of the warehouse only when danger reared its ugly head. As if.

Chapter Sixteen

I was glad to get back to London, if only for a rest. After the preceding week's events, the chaos of the dealing room was exactly what I needed – an honest atmosphere of greed, with nothing more supernatural than the grinning face of Mammon looming over everybody's shoulders. Michael was still excited about what had happened at Austen Hall, but this was based mainly upon his ignorance of what had occurred: his week had consisted mainly of preening, pretending to be lord of the manor and attempting to get any woman under forty alone long enough for what he considered an infallible method of seduction. The facts, especially the resistance of Miss Marsh to his advances, spoke against the infallibility of his arts, but he wasn't going to let that get in the way of his bragging. He was quite impressed by my apparent success with 'Miss Gentle', though. Since she had resisted his charms on a number of occasions, he was sticking with the conclusion he'd voiced before: that she was a lesbian. His feelings on the matter were entirely predictable: that homosexuality in men was repugnant and unnatural, but in women it was perfectly fine – as long as the women were attractive and he was allowed to watch.

I was looking forward to romancing 'Miss Gentle', a pseudonym that belied her true nature quite extraordinarily. For all her inexperience, and the obvious fact that women were second-class in their view, she'd done well to progress as far as she had within the Eagle Society, and if we could form a convincing couple it might well help her advance further. This was to be encouraged, since she would provide extra detail from a side of the organisation that was beyond any reasonable access for myself. But that was for later in the week, since we had agreed to meet on Thursday evening.

Monday evening was a more immediate priority. Sir James, previously known as Mr Gold, had invited me to dine at his club, where I was to receive instruction regarding my expanded responsibilities.

'As well as the money, we need you to get us some information. Our original plan's had to go by the board and now we need to improvise. How do you feel about a little light burglary?'

'No problem. What am I after?'

'Medical records. You'll be taking Folkestone with you, to make sure it's the right data, but he'll be the only person outside the circle who knows the subject's name. We can't risk trusting the troops with this, it's too important.'

'So where am I going?'

'Harley Street. The subject's GP is there, and you'll want to get everything he has. Take copies and leave the originals *in situ*. Oh, and make sure you're discreet about it, would you? We can't afford any slip-ups now, considering what's already gone wrong in the last week.

'You're going to be working more closely with Folkestone now, so you'd better try to get on with the fellow. We need a new man on security and you're going to be it. Folkestone's your link to the troops who, while they might have seen us at Austen Hall, don't really know who we are. Folkestone's how we keep it that way, so take care of him and he'll take care of you.'

'Right.' I'd have been delighted to take care of Folkestone, but I didn't think Sir James and I were using the same definition of the phrase.

But I was willing to call that a major win. Not only did I have the money, but with a penetration agent in charge of their security the outfit was now well on its way to destruction. Sir James passed me an envelope – the list of accounts through which the Society's money was filtered and deployed. Charities to collect it in, investments and dividends to slip it back out again without drawing too much attention. The Service was going to have a field day with this. A second envelope held a selection of newspaper clippings, which I'd have to sit down and read later, and a set of plans for a big old town house in the classical style – my target for the break-in.

The clippings told me all I needed to know about the object of our interest: Lord Peter Williams. Born Pitr Walesa in 1943, he'd been orphaned by the war and sent to England as part of the refugee programme before the Soviets had brought the Iron Curtain down across that end of Europe. Having left school at fifteen, he started working as an East End barrow-boy and by eighteen had owned his first barrow. Over the next ten years, he bought more pitches, more barrows and hired people to run them while he sat back and looked at ways to increase his holdings. Shops followed, and after some clever investments he started to diversify, buying and selling parts of his companies with ruthless dedication. His stated aim was to make sure that his kids never knew the pain or poverty he had experienced, and by the time his first son was born in 1966 he was already well on the way to his first million. His second son arrived three years later, as did his fifth million, and by the twenty-first century he was one of the country's richest men.

Now sixty-three, there were rumours that he was considering retiring due to ill heath – presumably why the Society wanted his medical records. He held a majority of his company's shares, but a quick cross-check indicated that members of the Society had invested individually in his company. Each of their holdings was carefully under the limit beyond which interests have to be declared. Adding those shares up, however, gave me a total that equated to ten per cent of Lord Williams' company, which could spell real trouble if it were suddenly to go downhill.

Just to add a certain humour to the thing, Lord Williams' company was named Eagle Holdings. You've got to laugh sometimes.

Folkestone was enthusiastic about the burglary when I briefed him the following evening. He seemed to have decided that he liked me, a prospect that made me feel a sudden violent need for a shower. Then again, keeping him close would be useful for the moment – and if he had any suspicions about Miss Marsh, there was a good chance he'd bring them to me first. While he wasn't authorised to know what had happened inside the circle during and after the ritual, he appeared to have the idea that I'd saved everyone, and with them the cause. If I had to be a psychopath's hero then I'd just have to put up with it, but I couldn't help wondering how much more impressed he'd be if he knew exactly how much I was really capable of. I got rid of that thought as quickly as I could: it said a little bit too much about me, and none of it was good.

Next came Wednesday, and a meeting at work.

'John, we've been looking over your trading records.'

'Really? Why?'

'Your client list, too. It makes interesting reading.'

'I'm just trying to do my best, Bob.' Bob was my current line manager, head of the trading floor and one of the people responsible for making sure that I played within the rules.

'We can see that. You've been very lucky, John. There are quite a few buys here that look risky, then come good not long afterwards. Anyone would think that you've been getting inside information.'

'How? It's not like I know anyone with access to that kind of thing.'

'Apparently not, but the compliance people are starting to get suspicious and the new clients you've been bringing in are individuals we don't want to risk tainting with scandal. For someone without connections, you've done exceptionally well there.'

'Word of mouth, Bob. You know how these people like to spread it about a bit, and I guess they want to ride my luck while it lasts.'

'Yes. They like to talk about it as well, and someone's obviously got the old man's ear. I've been told to promote you.'

'Oh.' That wasn't where I'd been expecting things to go.

'I can't say that I agree, or that I think you're ready, but I have to follow orders just like you. I'm supposed to give you a company car as well, but I think you'd rather not accept that. Don't you agree?'

'I suppose I do.' He was already unhappy, so giving him a bone wasn't a bad thing to do. It wasn't as if I couldn't get a car if I wanted one.

'Good. I'm going to be watching you, John. Something's not right, and I'm going to find out what it is before you get me into the shit. Every trade you make, I'll be watching. Now piss off before I find a reason to screw you out of your bonus.'

Penny Marsh at least had the decency to be sympathetic. She was stuck in what sounded like a hellish existence as a PA to some corporate bigwig, which had given her access to enough business information to make her useful from the Eagle Society's point of view. She'd already pulled a few bits of information from the corporate files, although luckily none of it was relevant to the trades I'd been making. This point made Bob's suspicions far more relevant, although I knew full well that my early successes on the floor had been down to the Service doing exactly the same thing. Between her bitching about her cover job and me bitching about mine, we managed to spend the entire evening talking without mentioning the actual job in hand once. It's something I can never quite get used to: two fake people talking about their fake lives despite the fact that they both know who the other is and what they really do for a living. Well, Penny didn't know *exactly* what I do for a living, but she had enough of an idea to meet the standard.

Dinner and bitching came to a close, and I offered to see her home. Given that we were theoretically taking it slowly, I wasn't sure what she'd say, but she was happy to leave me at her front door rather than the restaurant's. A swift phone call brought us a minicab, carefully swept, staffed and deployed by the Service. Oddly enough, she'd had a similar idea, although MI5 had set up a cab full of recording gear to make sure they caught anything I might let slip. I sent hers away, much to the obvious disgust of the driver, but this led me to a fairly important question.

'What have you told them about me? My mob know about you, obviously, but since you can't tell yours about me—'

'They think I've found an in with one of the command group and I'm exploiting it as best I can.'

'Sounds reasonable. Remind me to let you have the occasional thing to report back.'

'How about what happened out in the sticks?'

'Not quite what I had in mind, but still. There was a thing with psychedelics that went iffy, and three of the group had an allergic reaction.'

'Is that the best you can do? A bunch of highly respectable Nazi bastards tripping their tits off?'

'That's what I expect MI5 to think I told you, anyway. The truth is a little more complex.'

'And that is?'

'Classified.' This answer did not impress her, and it wouldn't have done much for me, either. 'I'm not going to tell you the whole story now, but once we're clear of it all I'll tell you what I can. Deal?'

'Do I have a choice?'

'Not really, but it's more than I should be offering.' That was true. I was going to have to work up a tale to tell her that would cover what she knew without letting her in on the bigger secret behind it. Although in all honesty I could probably have told her everything and she wouldn't have believed it. People don't, on the whole – apart from the nutters out on the fringe who think that the royal family are aliens, and who's going to believe them?

We got back to her place, where it was made very clear that coffee wasn't an option, and Penny left me with a kiss on the cheek and what sounded like genuine thanks for a good evening. I was happy with that – it fitted the profile we were building and I felt like we'd both actually had a pretty enjoyable evening. For me, it was a relief to be spending time with someone who didn't make me want to reach for a weapon, and I hoped she felt the same way in spite of the fact that she knew I wasn't being completely honest with her.

The journey home was a good chance to relax after that and find the right space for my head to be in. She was certainly beautiful, and smart, and funny, and all the other stuff you hope for in a woman, but she was still the help, and co-opted help at that. A little professional detachment goes a long way, especially when you've spent an evening pretending to be interested in an attractive woman who's spent the evening pretending very convincingly to be interested in you.

'Boss?' The driver's voice broke into my reverie. 'I think we've got company.'

'Who?'

'Silver Saab, about three cars back. He's not bad, but the turn outside your lady-friend's place flushed him out.'

'Anyone else?'

'Not that I can see. Either they know what they're doing or he's on his own.'

'What about losing him?'

'I could outrun him, but not without him spotting something fishy. This thing's supposed to be a two-litre, and he's got more horses than we should have.'

'Shit. Backstreets?'

'Only if you want him to know we've seen him.'

'Bollocks. All right, let's pretend he's not there, but see if you can pull him in for a closer look. I'd like a guess at who this bastard is, at least.'

So we sped up and slowed down, stopped at a cash machine and a garage, and generally made arses of ourselves in the hope of getting a chance at eyeballing our tail. Dark-blond hair, suntan, average-looking build but without much fat – not a great deal to work with, but I hoped I had enough detail to at least put a sketch together when I got home. He certainly knew what he was doing with the car, even though his tailing technique needed some work. The other thing we could be sure of was that he was on his own: a professional tailing team would have pulled him at regular intervals to break up the pattern while another car came in to take his place. That ruled out MI5, and the police, and any other official agency. I didn't recognise his face from the Eagle Society, either, so it was starting to look as though we had a new player joining the game. Like it wasn't enough of a pain in the arse already.

The cab dropped me at home and I watched my tail drive by as I opened the door. He was clocking my address and I was happy to get one more look at him. After a quick go at the sketch pad, I turned in. It was late, and I had a burglary to plan.

Chapter Seventeen

Folkestone's enthusiasm for the burglary continued through the research phase, as he cheerfully found specifications for the security systems that the doctor's place was known to have. He had good ideas during the planning, and was only too keen to help find the right equipment to get us in, through and out again. At one point he even offered to find an old spy camera for photographing documents, but I managed to convince him that a portable document scanner would be easier to work with. His dedication was absolute, and he wanted nothing more than to do the best job he could – despite the fact that we ended up having to wait two months for the right window of opportunity. The doctor in question kept hours that were best described as odd, and the only thing we could do was wait for the unco-operative old bastard to go on holiday.

Despite the delay, Folkestone still brought that same dedication to the burglary itself. Getting in was going to be a challenge, and we ended up using a fire escape five doors down to reach rooftop level. We worked quietly, methodically and as quickly as we could, soft-soled urban-assault boots gently lowered onto the metal steps of the fire escape to minimise noise, movements slow and easy so as not to draw the eye. For an amateur Folkestone was pretty good, and we were up top in less than ten minutes with no sign of any alarm having been called. The plans hadn't indicated any cameras on this approach and I was glad to see they'd been right. It was just a matter of making our way across the roofs to our target.

This was the first tricky part. We'd been lucky with the weather but that didn't make the walk any less hair-raising, keeping low on the roof so as to avoid being silhouetted against the sky. Even on dry slate, this was difficult – a matter of fine balance and good traction, since one slip would have ended the job fairly conclusively. Civilisation might have been grateful to see Folkestone's departure, but that would have left me with a lot of explaining to do in more than one direction, and still stuck four storeys up with little chance of getting down safely before the authorities showed up. We both had to make it through this alive, and get away with it, if I was to find out what was really going on. Why was this so important that I had to do it? If I were alone I might have thought the whole thing to be a possible set-up, but Folkestone's presence gave the job credibility – they wouldn't want to waste their chief enforcer simply to get rid of me when there were easier ways of doing so.

It took a good fifteen minutes to make the traverse, maintaining the stealth theme all the way, but we finally got to the skylight that was to be our access point into the building. It was easy enough to rig a bypass on the alarm sensor, and the lock wasn't much of a challenge, so we were through it quickly and into what the plans told us was a storeroom. Most of it was filled with boxes of paper – old patient notes and records. If Lord Williams had been dead, his records would quite probably have been in one of the boxes, but he wasn't so we had to head down.

There were three storeys beneath us, with our target two down on the first floor. The landing was deserted, this being one of the few buildings on the street that didn't have patient accommodation in-house. Still moving quietly, however, just in case. Up to the top of the stairs, and the first motion sensor. No point fannying about, so I unplugged it – we were coming out the same way so I could just plug it back in again afterwards. The landlord was noted as a cheap bastard in the briefing, so it wasn't exactly a surprise that he hadn't had the sense to fit an alarm that registered sudden equipment failures. Down the stairs and around the landing, disabling another sensor on the way, then down to the first floor for a repeat prescription.

Next up was the door into the consulting rooms, solidly built and fitted with a decent lock. A mortise, luckily for me: just a matter of finding the lever pattern and one full rotation to get it open. The rotation's a pain, but it's better than the sprung workings that snap you back the moment something slips. Folkestone's excitement was starting to work against him now, as he had to stand and wait while I felt my way around the inside of the lock, finding the pattern that I needed to open it up. This takes patience and concentration, two qualities that are not aided by six feet of muscle almost bouncing with anticipation next to you. At least he had the sense to keep his gob shut.

These things always seem to be going nowhere when I do them, then suddenly it all fits together and I'm through. One quick turn of the wrist and we were in.

Streetlamps outside the window were enough to see by. We were in the waiting room, wood-panelled, expensively furnished and decorated with the occasional print. Two doors led out, besides the one we'd just come through, and since one had the doctor's name on it we decided to try the other one first.

A kitchen and a bathroom. Ah well, I can't get it right every time.

So the doctor's office had to be our destination. Locked again, but defeated just as easily. To be honest, there's no such thing as an impenetrable lock, just locks that make getting past them so difficult that it's not worth the trouble. This was not one of those – it was a token lock for the purpose of telling people not to come in and not much more. A decent locksmith would have been through it even faster than me.

The doctor's office faced out towards the back of the building, where light was in much shorter supply. Time for a torch – the lens covered with gaffer tape that had a couple of holes in it to let out a thin stream of light. Enough to work by, but not so much that it would be noticed by anyone looking at the window. You'd be surprised how obvious a torch beam can be inside an otherwise darkened room, even when the beam's nowhere near the window.

Filing cabinets: just what we wanted. Three of the things lined up against the wall next to the door, each one with a shiny lock in the top right-hand corner. Folkestone was on those in a heartbeat, eager to show that he could pull his weight at least a little on this run. As he opened the locks, I started checking drawers. We started at the bottom right, on the theory that 'W' is nearer the end of the alphabet than the beginning, and found a bottle of scotch. It was nice to know that some traditions continue, even if the good doctor was unlikely to share it with his patients.

The file was in the top right, neatly hanging on its rails and full of papers – I was glad I'd brought the largest memory card I could find. I set Folkestone to scanning the documents as I handed them to him and collected them back together once he was done. Even at ten seconds a sheet we were at it for an hour, and that bottle of scotch was starting to look tempting. But time was a-wasting. We locked the file away, secured the office and made our way back up the stairs, remembering to reconnect everything as we went. Then it was out of the skylight to discover rain.

It had been bad enough crossing that roof when it was dry, but now there was the added danger that came with wet slate. To call it slippery would be one hell of an understatement, and I almost lost my footing more than once. If Folkestone hadn't been there I would have been pavement pâté, and he seemed glad to have a chance to prove his worth again. Under the circumstances I was more than happy to let him, too.

Down the fire escape – also more than a little slippery – and into the alley, then out and into the van we'd left waiting. Heaters full on, we vanished into the night.

'That was amazing!' Folkestone had obviously enjoyed himself. 'Have you done a lot of that, sir?'

'Not really, but I've climbed a couple of mountains. I wouldn't have minded some ropes up on the roof, to be honest.'

'You're all right, sir, I'll look after you. Part of the job, that.'

'Then you earned your pay tonight. Are you going to be OK delivering that scanner?'

'No problem, sir.'

'Good. Then drop me at home, would you? I've got work in the morning.'

Folkestone dropped me around the corner from my place, since there was a van blocking the car park's entrance. I checked it for recognition marks automatically, but it looked like just another anonymous white van making a delivery – the side door open and engine running. Begging to be nicked, but you can't tell some people. I made a point of stepping away from the door out of habit, just in case, but the figure that barrelled into me from the building entrance carried me straight into it anyway. There was a pad over my mouth, something thick and sweet-smelling inside it. Then the world went black.

My first thought was that I'd been picked up by the Service for a late-night debrief, but the cable ties securing my wrists made that pretty unlikely. I was alone in the back of the van, which had been lined with boards in such a way as to make sure there was nothing for me to get a grip on or use to try to get free. As the van moved I was thrown about inside, and with no windows or way to look at my watch I had no idea how long I'd been unconscious. No idea either about where we were going. This was not looking good.

I'd been awake for what felt like an hour when we finally stopped moving. There was a rattle from outside, the sound of a shutter closing, then the door opened and I received a solid punch on the nose as a greeting. Not enough to break it, but there was a bit of blood and I was sufficiently disorientated for my kidnapper to get that pad over my face again.

Back to the waking world, and I was in a chair. My wrists and ankles were attached to it, but I was surprised to discover that I still had clothes on. Not a professional interrogation, then, so what was going on? It looked as if the man was acting on his own – he'd certainly operated that way during the pickup, where I would have used a couple of extra bodies if they were available to me. Not the Society, then, or at least not officially. If my cover had been blown I'd have expected a decent operation, probably with Folkestone driving me straight to the rendezvous while I thought everything was still fine. MI5 would have done something similar, at least in manpower, whether or not Penny was involved. No, this was someone else, a new player. I'd thought things were going too bloody well.

A set of lights came on, all pointed at me. Very traditional. I could make out a figure at their edge – tall, well muscled and looking at me. I resisted the urge to make a smart-arse comment: the first trick is not to start talking.

'What is your name?' The accent was German, very clipped. Educated, too – the kind of voice you used to hear a lot in old war movies. I couldn't suppress the idea of him telling me that my war was over, and fought hard to hide the grin. It doesn't do to piss people off when you're tied to a chair – they have way too many options when it comes to explaining their displeasure.

'My name is Heinrich. Why not tell me yours?' Because I see no reason to start a conversation, that's why. I kept my mouth shut.

'Look, I do not want to hurt you. Just tell me your name.' This was getting dull. I let him ask me a few more times while I ran a couple of ideas through. If he was on his own he'd need to take a break, and if he left me alone I'd have a chance at escape. That chance would be better if I was intact, so it might be worth playing him a bit.

'William Holliday.'

'And what do your friends call you, William – "Doc"?'

'Billy.' I look nothing like her, but it was the first thing that came to mind.

'Billy Holliday. Should I be blue for you?' He was referencing a Miles Davis number rather than anything Lady Day sang, but I had to give him points for catching it.

'If you want.'

'No, Mr Dennis. You see, I asked the manager of the restaurant where you had dinner with that lovely young lady. He was only too happy to help me work out if I had seen my old friend Anders, but instead you turned out to be someone else entirely. So why do you lie to me? I am trying to be your friend.'

'You haven't been all that friendly so far.'

'Ah, but I could be so much less friendly. All I want you to do is tell me about your friends, the ones you went to the country with. I would also like to know what happened to my friend Paul. He went to the country too, but has not come back yet.'

'How would I know anything about that?'

'Because he was taking your photographs, and I think you must have noticed him.' Oh great – he was connected to Penny's journalist. Telling Heinrich that I'd watched his friend tortured to the point of insanity wasn't likely to go down well, especially in my current situation. It was also a fine argument against having let Folkestone play his little game with the guy. I had no idea where the remains had ended up, but I doubted that there'd ever be more than a token funeral.

'I don't know anything about that. Security was someone else's department.'

'Really? Whose?' This is why you don't start talking. One question leads to another and before you know it you're in trouble.

'I don't know his real name, just his colour.'

'Very wise. That way you cannot tell someone like me who they are, can you?'

'I imagine that's the general idea.'

'Hmm. You will tell me everything you know, I think. One way or another.'

'Why? What's your angle here?'

'Apart from finding my friend? I think your friends have killed him, John. So now I have two reasons to knock your little club out, and two reasons to celebrate when I do.'

'What's the other reason, then?' That got a brief smile.

'My grandfather. You are aware of the camps, yes?'

'He was in one?'

'In a manner of speaking. I idolised him, you see. I knew that he had fought in the war, and won medals for bravery, but we did not really talk about it. He died five years ago, and a journalist came to ask the family what we thought about his war record. We were proud, of course, that he had been a brave soldier who fought for his country, but to us he was just Grandpa Willi. Ah, says the journalist, but what about the camps?'

'What about them?'

'Grandpa Willi, it turned out, had not been in the Army but the SS. When he was wounded, they transferred him to Dachau so he could recover before returning to the front. He knew what was going on there, and helped to do it. There were papers, proving that he did these things.'

'What does that have to do with me?'

'Because he dishonoured our family! Because he followed that disgusting little Austrian! Because you and your friends want it to happen again! People like you need to be stopped, so that evil stays dead and buried where it belongs!'

I couldn't exactly argue with logic like that. If his story was true then I had a great deal of sympathy for this poor bastard, even if he needed to work on his methods and find some backup. There were groups out there sympathetic to his cause, and he would have done better to swallow his pride and work with them.

'So why are you working alone?'

No answer.

'Oh, come on, it's obvious that you haven't got any help here. A one-man tail, a one-man kidnapping – if you had help you would have used it.'

'Why? I have managed to capture you, have I not?'

'You got lucky.'

'No, I just planned it properly. Now I am going to let you think about what I have said, and when I come back you will tell me everything you know – a full confession. After that I shall give you to the police, along with your confession. You will agree that this is a far more pleasant scenario than the one likely to take place if our positions were reversed, yes?'

'I'm sure of it.'

'Good.' And with that, he turned away and stepped out of the light. 'But think for a moment, Mr Dennis, on what I have said. Confess and repent, and all will be well.'

He did a good job closing the door, but the acoustics were against him and I just made out the sound of the latch sliding back into its hole in the door frame. I couldn't see anything outside the lights' harsh glare, but there wasn't anything to lose by having a crack at getting free. The cable ties he'd used to attach me to the chair were a type I recognised – I'd used the same model myself for a while, but given them up because of an unfortunate weakness in the catch that was supposed to hold them closed. That weakness had almost got me killed when a subject I was sitting on slipped free and tried to take my eye out with a chair leg, and now it was going to pay me back. Just a matter of twisting my wrist to the right angle – painful but possible – and applying the correct amount of pressure . . .

Click. A couple of notches passed through the grip. Excellent news. Now all I had to do was repeat it. I clenched my fist to tense the muscles and re-establish the pressure, and twisted again. It cost me a layer of skin, but gave me some more room. The third twist drew blood, but now the tie was just loose enough to let my hand slip through. With that hand free, releasing my other wrist was a speedier process. With both hands, the ankles were a piece of cake since I could just angle the ties with my fingers. I stood up and headed into the darkness.

No response from my German friend, so I cast about to see if I could spot the contents of my pockets. There, on the table, coming into focus as my eyes adjusted to the lower light level. I was just finishing putting things back where they belonged when Heinrich returned.

'Now, Mr Dennis, shall we– *Scheisse!*' I charged straight at him, head down. Hard skull met soft midriff, throwing him back against the wall and making a very satisfying crack as his skull bounced back off the brickwork. He did a fine impersonation of a sack of spuds, sliding down the wall as he took a nap of his own.

No time to waste. I checked his pockets, found his passport and committed the number to memory: Heinrich von Oderbar, unless the passport was a *very* good forgery. Then it was out to the van and, courtesy of Heinrich's keys, away from the place as quickly as possible. After ten minutes of driving around aimlessly I found my way off the industrial estate – which was in the middle of a normal business day by then – and headed back to London, pausing only to grab a sandwich and call in sick. I needed a lie down.

Chapter Eighteen

I had a couple of options as far as Heinrich was concerned: I could drop him in it with the Eagle Society, which meant death: hand him off to the Service, which would be deportation if he was lucky but quite possibly death: or I could let him be for a bit and see if he might come in useful, which could also get him killed but might do me some good at the same time. Given that I could have killed him at the warehouse and didn't, getting someone else to do it for me seemed like a shitty thing to do. But why hadn't I done the obvious thing? Probably because I sympathised with his story. If it was true, then I could understand how a childhood hero turning out bad had unhinged the bugger. At least he'd found something constructive to do with his anger, which is more than most people would manage. I decided to run a check on him and make up my mind what to do once I had some more information.

I was approaching the anniversary of my insertion, too, and to be honest the job was starting to get to me. I couldn't really complain – I'd done spectacularly well in the previous twelve months and was looking at wrapping the show up in only a couple more. But I was really going to need a holiday after this, somewhere quiet where I could piss around with my guitars and forget about the whole business for a while. Maybe I'd take Penny Marsh along, and prove that I wasn't just some robot who did nothing but work. Not a realistic idea, that one, but amusing nonetheless. Seriously, though, there would have to be some downtime after I wrapped up the Eagle Society, no matter what the Boss said. Too much of this crap can drive you mad.

With Ffoulkes back on deck, if a little shaky, there was a meeting planned for the remaining nine members of the circle later that same week. With all of us seated at the round table, four empty chairs representing the casualties from Austen Hall, it was all very Arthurian – but then Himmler had had his round table of thirteen as well, and I couldn't help wondering exactly which of the two was a bigger influence in the room whether it was stated or not.

'Thanks to Mr Dennis, with Folkestone's able assistance, we now have Lord Williams' medical records.' Sir James had gone straight to business this time, with only the most basic of opening bullshit. 'And the news is exactly as we were led to believe. According to his doctor, Lord Williams will be dead in about five years. His cancer is spreading very slowly at the moment and responding to therapy, but the long-term odds of survival are very poor indeed – if the disease doesn't get him, the treatments will. In short, we have a perfect scenario from which to progress. And progress we shall!' There was a round of applause, and I joined in without a clue what the man was talking about.

'Of course, the obstacle remains in place at the present time, but I think that after their previous success I'm going to suggest that Mr Dennis and Folkestone take care of it for us. Agreed?' Nods of assent. 'I also think that it's long past the point where Mr Dennis should have been more fully briefed on the overall situation, having joined our company after the initial planning was completed. He's taken a great deal on faith and served us very well even in his blindness, so unless there are any objections I propose to explain the situation to him fully after this meeting is concluded. Does anybody object?' Far from it: there were comments of the 'good show' variety from around the table. Administrative business was dealt with quickly, and the meeting adjourned for drinks. Being the kind of outfit it was, I had to put up with claps on the shoulder and welcoming words for a bit before Sir James tapped me on the arm and led me to a side room. At last it was time to find out exactly what the bastards had in mind.

'We really can't thank you enough, John.' We were in arm-chairs, a glass of scotch each and a cigar for Sir James. Somehow I thought that the smoking ban was never going to have much pull in the lands of the mighty, since the rich make their own laws to begin with. 'You've worked hard, and we appreciate you putting up with Michael. How's he doing, by the way?'

'He can't be bothered to read and does everything he can to avoid talking about the tutoring, let alone showing up for it.' I was grateful for that, since he was enough of an arse at work that I didn't relish spending time outside the office with him as well.

'I can't say I'm surprised, really. He's nothing like his father. We were in the Guards together, you know. Splendid fellow: never shirked, complained or missed a chance to move the cause forward. Frankly we're all a little disappointed in young Michael.'

'I can see why.'

'I'm sure you can, John. I'm sure you can. But that's why you've been such a godsend – you've made a real difference to our circle, and not just by preventing things from becoming more unpleasant back at the Hall. With the vacancies left by our fallen brothers-in-arms, it's been decided that you should be offered a permanent place rather than just standing in for Michael. He can take his place when – if – he's ready, but to lose your talents because of it would be foolish at best. Congratulations.'

'Thank you, I'm honoured.'

'An honour you earned, my boy. And since you're properly

one of us now, it's time you were told of our plan: the means by which we intend to make Britain great again, and reassume our proper place in world affairs.

'Lord Williams – Pitr Walesa – well, you read the file. But there are more details that aren't publicly known. You see, he wasn't an orphan when he was relocated, but his parents were officially dead. It was decided, for his own safety, to relocate him to England so that he'd be well looked after among friends while his parents went into hiding. If everything had gone according to plan he would have been told the truth at the appropriate time, the truth we've been keeping secret for sixty years, but a British agent managed to bring everything down, and so the decision was taken to keep his background a secret until the time was right. We believe that the time is approaching when his heritage can be brought to Britain's aid, and that is the plan we are in the process of enacting.

'You see, John, Lord Williams' actual parents were Eva Braun . . . and Adolf Hitler.'

'You've got to be kidding.' That was putting it mildly. 'That's too big a secret to keep quiet.'

'Not even he knows this. You are now the eleventh person alive with this information. It's been held by the Society and one other – the chairman of the organisation that provides financial and other arrangements for us. We are largely self-sufficient, but he allows us access to other means of support around the world.'

'So what's the other organisation?'

'It was set up by Martin Bormann during the last days of the war. Money, information, personnel . . . Everything needed to allow the leaders of the Third Reich to escape. They provided the bodies burned outside the bunker, and made sure that no one lived to tell that they were not Adolf and Eva Hitler. Afterwards they found their way into government service all over the world – in the CIA, MI5 and MI6, in Spain, France, Italy and

South America. We have friends everywhere, John.'

'Like ODESSA, then?'

'No. ODESSA was a blind to allow other groups to operate, although some of the people attached to it provided a suitable distraction that gave us a chance to smuggle the survivors out of Europe and made sure that the child was moved to a suitably safe location.'

The Bormann Organisation. Rumours about it still echoed around after all these years, and what little I knew about it tied up with what Sir James was telling me. They weren't strictly within my remit, but if I could get a handle on them the dividends we could gain would be extraordinary. Quite a few people were still very interested in finding out solid information about them, and that information could be used very easily to our advantage. It was another excellent reason to start following the money before we took the Eagle Society down.

'So what are we going to do next?'

'Lord Williams is dying, so we're turning our attention to the younger generation. His own children are useless – wasteful, stupid, spineless peons. But his eldest grandson Henry is a much better specimen. He's still young, but he's good-looking, charming and very clever indeed. It is our intention that he should inherit his grandfather's holdings and use them to enter politics, from which position he will be able to subvert the system from inside and bring a decent government back into power. There are other advantages we intend to supply him with, but more of that another time.'

'What about his father?'

'Yes, well, that's where you and Folkestone are going to help things along. Given that the other son has an unfortunate habit of putting things up his nose that's about to go rather wrong, Jonathan Williams also needs to be removed from the succession in time to allow everyone to get used to the new status quo. It's been decided that acting now will allay suspicion of the situation being manipulated, and ensure that nobody suspects the boy when he comes into his inheritance.'

'You want me to kill him.'

'Yes.'

'In any particular manner?'

'Whatever you feel most appropriate, but make sure it doesn't attract any more attention than can be avoided.'

'I'm sure we'll come up with something.'

'As am I. But make it a clean death if you can – none of Folkestone's little embellishments. Jonathan is still of the blood and that deserves a certain amount of respect.'

'I'll work up a plan, then. Is there a preferred timescale?'

'As soon as is practical.'

'Right.'

This was no problem at all. Wiping out this bloodline was a public service to begin with, and if I could get away with it under the Society's blessing I was happy to do it. The Service wasn't likely to have a problem with it either.

'Is this related to the ritual that went wrong?'

'Yes, but that part of the plan will be explained later. One thing at a time, John.'

One thing at a time, indeed. What did trying to get Hitler out of Hell have to do with putting his great-grandson in charge of the British government? It had to be something pretty impressive if they were keeping it secret even after telling me what they had. Finding out would be interesting, and the Boss was going to love my next report.

'They want you to do *what?*' Penny Marsh's response was entirely predictable. We'd had another evening together that had gone really well, and we were starting to get along as people. She'd even laughed with me when I told her about my manager Bob being fired, presumably for kicking up a fuss over my promotion from the way he looked daggers at me on his way out. The chance to depressurise a little was doing both of us good, right up to the point when I decided to tell her what was going on at my end of the operation.

'They want me to kill Jonathan Williams.'

'And you're actually going to do it?'

'Yep.'

'But you can't!'

'Why not?'

'It's illegal! This country's Security Services don't murder people just to stay in an enemy's good books.'

'We do under circumstances like these.'

'Then tell me what the circumstances are, at least.'

'My Service has a standing order that covers this: if any descendents of Adolf Hitler are discovered, they are to be eliminated. It's a holdover from someone being careful after the war.'

'Right. So who gave the order?'

'Churchill.'

'Oh.'

'And it was ratified by the King. Will that do you?'

'No, not really. But it's not like I have any input, is it?'

'Not in this case. I have to follow the order, and by choosing the way in which I do it I can turn it into leverage with the Eagle Society. Everybody wins.'

'Except Jonathan Williams.'

'And the rest of his family, eventually. But they're screwed anyway – now the information's in our hands it has to be acted on.'

'Jesus. Just when I start thinking of you as a human being you pull something like this out of the bag. Won't you at least check first?'

'There'll be a quiet DNA test on the body, certainly.'

'You mean you haven't got some kind of secret database with everybody's DNA in it?'

'I wish. The government put the bloody thing out to tender, so it might be up and running by about the twenty-third century if we're lucky.' That got a laugh.

'So you lot are as stuffed as the rest of us.'

'We're still part of the Civil Service, Penny, so sometimes even we get hosed.'

Folkestone, on the other hand, was somewhat less concerned about the idea. His only disappointment was the need for discretion. We spent a Sunday afternoon going over options that ranged from exotic poisons to old-fashioned bombs until we ended up with a solution that would do what was needed.

The next weekend saw Jonathan Williams playing with cars. He was more than a little fond of the playboy lifestyle and had been living it up pretty solidly since his divorce two years previously. Models, nightclubs and racing seemed to be his major things, and the third was the in that we decided would work best. All we needed was some high-octane racing fuel, a plastic bag and thirty seconds with the car. It was a piece of cake to impersonate a member of his pit crew for that long, with all the running around and preparation before the start, and we dropped the half-filled bag of fuel on top of his engine and closed the bonnet. With that done, all we had to do was change back into civvies and watch the race.

As Jonathan shot around the track, science was working for us. The heat of the engine warmed the fuel in the bag, turning it into vapour. As more fuel vaporised, the pressure in the bag increased. Eventually the bag popped, spraying hot fuel vapour all over the engine, which was in turn hot enough to ignite it. The front half of the car basically exploded, then the fuel in the tank kept on feeding the fire. Simple, elegant and all evidence destroyed – not that anyone would be looking for the remains of a thin plastic bag to begin with.

One Hitler down, three to go.

Chapter Nineteen

Things were starting to come together. I had a pretty good idea of what the Eagle Society was up to, and how they were planning to do it. I still just about had Penny Marsh under control, and the money was being traced back to start getting a handle on the Bormann Organisation. I still had Heinrich, whose file had come back clean and verified the story he told me, to deal with, but as long as he stayed out of my direct line of fire I was inclined to leave him be. I'd not seen any sign of him since our little chat and was hoping that he'd decided to play it clever and keep his head down for a bit.

At the circle's next meeting I got a round of applause for Jonathan Williams' 'accident' and another clue about what else was happening.

'Preparations for Phase Two are proceeding well,' said Sir James. 'Arrangements are being made for the transfer of necessary equipment to Germany, and our contact has ensured that we won't be disturbed. All that remains is for the last few pieces of apparatus to be acquired and delivered to the staging point. You all have one or two items to obtain and a recommended supplier, so I expect this to proceed easily within the next week.'

We were indeed each issued with a piece of paper, upon which were the details of what we had to get. Mine was simple – the skulls of two murderers. All I had to do was pop up to Manchester, collect them and bring them back to London. A refreshingly easy job, given what they'd had me doing of late. Then I noticed the address: Benjamin Daniels, 23 Saddlesby Street.

Fuck.

Benjamin Eustace bloody Daniels.

Benny and I were acquainted, and there was no way it could be described as a close friendship. The last time I'd seen him I'd had cause to beat eight bells out of him and threaten to crush his hand in an old mangle. I'd been good enough to empty his till so he'd have an easy explanation for the police, but I doubted that would be much use for keeping him on side.

'I thought you deserved the easy one.' Sir James had come up behind me while I was boggling at the paper – not a good thing. 'Why not take Miss Gentle and make a weekend of it?'

'Manchester's not exactly the first place I think of for a romantic getaway.'

'Then stop off on the way back from somewhere else. The two of you deserve some time together without the rest of us getting in the way. I'd be happier with your cargo having an escort anyway, even if she doesn't know what it is.'

Not a chance. The last thing I needed was her knocking around if things went pear-shaped with Benny.

'Is she really suitable for that?'

'No, I suppose not. Oh well, serves me right for being a romantic. Take Folkestone instead; you can do the trip in a day and take Miss Gentle out on the Sunday.'

Way to go, Jack. You just turned a milk run into a life-threatening situation.

Saturday dawned, and Folkestone met me at the station. The journey passed easily enough, with talk of music, life and the world in general. In many ways Folkestone came across as an alright bloke, so playing along wasn't too difficult. In another life

I might even have come to like him – were he not a psychopathic Nazi, anyway. We grabbed some lunch at a café near the station, then made our way into the backstreets to hunt for Benny's shop.

It was no different from the last time I'd been there, about eighteen months before. Yellow plastic still lined the windows and the faded paint above the door was completely illegible, suggesting a name purely by the vague shapes of what were probably letters put there when the Romans had landed. It was the kind of place that respectable people avoided like a leper colony, and that was just the way Benny liked it. His only regular visitors were policemen looking for stolen antiques and people like us in search of esoteric bits and bobs you couldn't get anywhere else.

It was much the same inside, too: teetering piles of dusty crap that held thousands of pounds' worth of art and antiquities that most museums would kill for. He'd stick the occasional piece in for auction when he needed extra cash, and the word on the street was that he was doing a roaring trade online, but most of what could be seen was just to make the place look untidy enough that even a dedicated browser would take one look and decide not to bother. The mangle was still there, just where it had been during our last encounter, and it was that which held my attention as Benny came out of the back.

'What can I do for you, gentlemen?' His soft voice was at odds with his appearance – short, squat and ugly as sin. As I turned towards him his face went a little pale, but he held it together pretty well, considering.

'My name is Scarlett,' I told him, with a look that promised dire consequences if he decided to argue the point. 'You have something for me.'

'Um, yeah. Yes, I do.'

'Where is it?'

'It's just in the back. Have I met you before, Mr Scarlett?' The little scrote was trying it on. He was known as a sharp customer and must have twigged that I didn't want our previous association to be brought to Folkestone's attention.

'No, I don't think you have. I'm quite sure of it, in fact.' I let my eyes fall on the mangle again for a moment, enough to make him look at it and think back to what happened the last time he tried screwing me around. He was walking with a limp these days, quite possibly a souvenir from that unpleasant afternoon, and my hope was that he'd see it as a bloody good reason to behave rather than a reason to try and get his own back.

'As you say, Mr Scarlett.' He started shuffling towards the back room. 'Would you mind giving me a hand? I don't walk so well these days – must be old age catching up with me.'

I nodded and followed him, motioning to Folkestone that he should wait where he was.

'So, "Mr Scarlett" – or should I call you Chapman? This *is* a pretty little pinch you're in, isn't it?' Benny's tone had changed from his usual cringing deference into something nastier. 'What do you think would happen if I told your friend about that, eh?'

'Things would get very messy, Benny. Very messy indeed.'

'I bet they would. I bet he doesn't know who you work for, does he?'

'Nor do you.'

'No, but I've got an idea. Sneaking around looking for people, chasing artefacts? You're something official, that much I do know. Why should I cover for you?'

'Because if you don't I'll convince that nice man out front that you're trying to set us up, and then he'll be very angry with you. He's a creative bastard, that one, and he loves his work. Worst case, I'll have to kill him – and then I'll have to kill you to cover it up. But I'll take my time about it, Benny. You think I was nasty last time? If you make me get nasty again I'll take a Black and Decker to the back of your knees and be sure to do it *slowly*.'

'Oh.' His voice had shrunk again and there was fear in his eyes.

'And then I'll really go to town on you. So be a good boy, Benny, and I'll forget we had this little chat. I'll go away nice and quietly and you can get back to whatever it is you do in that grotty flat of yours upstairs. Right?'

'Right.'

'Good. Now give me the fucking package before I break your nose on general principle.'

Folkestone was starting to get restless as we came back out.

'Everything all right, Mr Scarlett?'

'It's fine. We just had a little trouble getting it out from under a pile.' Given the state of the rest of the shop this was not difficult to believe. 'So what do you have for us, Mr Daniels?'

'Ah,' said Benny. 'The very best for you gents: two skulls, both from a South American death squad. Shot by their own friends, too, so they're both murderers and murder victims. Two for the price of one-and-a-half.'

'The price has already been agreed.' I couldn't believe it – he was still going to try it on.

'But this is better than what you ordered – more uses. Best quality.'

'As I said, Mr Daniels, the price has been agreed.' I put an envelope full of money on the counter. 'I suggest you wrap them up and let us be on our way.'

'How much more?' asked Folkestone.

'Another thousand.'

'Fine.' Folkestone pulled out an envelope of his own and put it next to mine. 'Mr Gold was expecting this. Now do as Mr Scarlett says, before someone loses their temper.' That worked fine for Benny, who had obviously been considering my warning.

'Right you are, gents. I'll even throw in a bag for you.'

'Good man,' said Folkestone.

We were out a few minutes later, into air that smelled as fresh as you'd find in the country. You don't notice just how much of a dump Benny's shop is until you step outside again – sure, it's grimy and dusty, but there's an air about the place that creeps up on you at the same time. I blame the crap he keeps out back for people like me.

'What was all that about, then?'

'Hmm?' We were on the train back to London, and I wasn't really listening.

'With the old bloke. What was that in the back room?'

'He was trying to put the squeeze on us, trying to get more money. I told him what might happen if he didn't remember his manners.'

'Why worry? It's not like we don't have the money.'

'For a start you didn't mention that you had more on you, and there's the principle of the thing to consider as well. If we roll over once, who's to say he won't try it again next time?'

'What next time? Sir James says that once we've fixed this we won't have to worry about anything else for a long while – just sit back and let nature take its course.'

'Still, it's the principle. I don't like being pissed around like that.'

'You should have said. We could have gone back and explained the facts of life to him.'

'Too late now. At least we got what we went for.'

'Are you sure? I've got mates in Manc who'd be glad to take care of him for us.'

'Save the favour, it won't do any good now. They'd have to identify who they were working for, and that would mean they'd have to kill him to protect us. Let him have his money – I'll knock it off the next thing we have to get from him.'

'S'pose. Sorry if I cramped your style, though. It's just that I had orders – get in, pay him what he wanted and get out again, nice and quiet.'

'In that case you did the right thing. Shouldn't worry about it if I were you.'

Nice and quietly. Yeah, right – Benny bloody Daniels was now in a position to drop me quite thoroughly in the shit. I made a mental note to have someone pay him a visit.

Chapter Twenty

'A month from today, gentlemen, Phase Two will reach its fruition. With that, we will be considerably closer to our long-term goal.' Sir James was holding forth from the top of the table, obviously buoyed up by the successes that had come since the failed ritual. 'Travel plans are already set, and our contact at the ritual site is ensuring that we will not be disturbed when the time comes. Up until now it has been wiser to keep many of these details secret, but I believe this is an appropriate point for us to put the necessary cover stories into play.

'Each of us will be travelling separately, to a number of locations: Bonn, Cologne, Essen and so on. You are advised to find business reasons to be there – those who cannot plan their own itineraries will be found clients and such to give them reason to travel. You will complete your business by the Thursday and take the Friday off to go sightseeing. Your sightseeing trips will take you to Westphalia, where you will spend the Friday night in accommodation designated for the purpose. On the Saturday morning, you will be transported to the city of Büren, where you will prepare yourselves. Then, three hours before sunset, we will meet at a particular café. An hour later we will make our way to the ritual site. This will allow us one hour in which to prepare for the ritual and commence at sunset.'

'Why there?' I figured it was worth asking, even though the answer was one I expected.

'Because we have arranged to perform our ritual at a strong-point of power. A place sacred to those in whose footsteps we are following. We will be using the vault at Wewelsburg Castle.'

Great. If there was one place the SS thought of as sacred, it was Wewelsburg. The triangular castle overlooking the village that bore its name was nominated by Himmler himself to be the centre of his so-called knightly order and would, had we lost the war, have been his answer to the Vatican. The chamber that Sir James was talking about was thought to have been sacred to the dead, and possibly the place where senior SS men's ashes were to be interred. Twelve pedestals, a place for the eternal flame, and all the twisted imagery we could need for some very nasty shit to go down.

'The objective for this ritual is to make contact once again with the soul of Adolf Hitler. The child has been told that as part of his ascension he is to be blessed by the late Führer, but that is not the case. Using another form of the ritual attempted at Austen Hall, we will release the Führer from his prison and enable him to take possession of the child's body. Using the position of wealth and power he will then inherit from Lord Williams, his entry into and success in politics will be inevitable and this country will have the strong leadership it needs to take us forward into Europe and back to the position of global power that is not just our birthright but a necessary function for the security of all nations.' His voice was climbing now, the ranting really starting to show. 'Our friends in politics, in business, in all corners of the world will rise to our banner. Together we will obliterate the forces that seek to cause chaos, and establish a new order that will enforce stability, prosperity and solid moral values for all. Our armies will bring an end to war, our industrial might will provide employment, our spiritual guidance will end the falsehood of religion and together, my friends, together we will bring the world into a new golden age!'

He was expecting applause at this point, and he got it. Sir James waited patiently, letting the first wave die down a little before delivering the punchline.

'The Thousand-Year Reich did not die, my friends, it is merely sleeping. But we shall awaken it once more! The British lion shall roar it back from slumber, and all the peoples of the world shall hear it! We will not be stopped! We *cannot* be stopped! This is destiny – not ours, but the world's!'

I've heard some lunatic shit in my time, but Sir James was rapidly moving up the league table. It's always the quiet ones.

Rhetoric is a great motivator, but without logistics it won't get you very far. Each of us received more orders, a sealed packet with the Eagle Society's insignia pressed into red wax on the flap and our names on the front. I was to be responsible for moving the ritual gear across to Germany from London, not a glamorous job but one that gave me an awful lot of information about how things were likely to run. The one thing sadly lacking was the name of our contact inside the castle, a connection we would need just to get us through the gates – let alone secure the privacy necessary to pull off a full-on ritual. There was enough there, though, for me to build a fair picture of the arrangement and start coming up with suitably innocuous-looking options that could prevent things from moving forward without giving away my hand in it.

I also had an ace in the hole, and this looked like the perfect time to use it.

'Heinrich von Oderbar. How nice to see you again.' When Heinrich's file had come back, it included the two addresses he was operating from. Just for a change, the world was on my side and the first one came up trumps – considering I'd only picked the flat because it was a damned sight more comfortable than the warehouse, this was one I was happy to chalk up in the 'lucky' column.

'How did you ... What are you doing here?' This reaction can go on for a bit if you let it, but Heinrich, to his credit, was dealing with it pretty well. Well enough to be slowly going for a weapon. Pointing a gun at him was a tacky thing to do, but it dissuaded him from being an idiot so I let myself get away with it.

'Sit down, Heinrich, it's Christmas.'

He did as he was told, fixing me with a terribly superior look that screamed aristocracy. Considering the ease with which he did it, he was either egomaniacal to the point of uselessness, accustomed to having guns pointed at him or sitting near another concealed weapon. My money was on the latter two.

'Christmas, indeed? Have you come to turn yourself in?'

'Not quite, but I am going to give you a way to hurt the Eagle Society.'

'Why?'

'It suits my purposes to do so. You don't need to know any more than that, and it wouldn't do you any good if you did.'

'You will understand if I am suspicious.'

'I'd be surprised if you weren't. But I'm going to give you a means to hurt their grand project in such a way that others can stop it completely.'

'What if I refuse?'

'Then I'm afraid I'll have to kill you. You've seen my face, and now that you know I'm willing to sell out, you represent a danger to me.'

'Then I can just agree to cooperate and deal with things after you leave.'

'You could, but then I'd kill you and your sister.'

'I see.' He paused, thinking for a moment. 'Perhaps if you were to put down the gun—'

'You'd pull the one you've got hidden in that chair and I'd be fucked.'

'Then it appears you are not giving me a choice.'

'None at all. It makes negotiating easier.'

'Quite. What is it you want me to do?'

'The Eagle Society will be moving certain items of equipment to a warehouse in Büren. The arrangements at that end are being made by their local contact, who is known to have an involvement with Wewelsburg Castle.' That got his attention. 'What I want you to do, Heinrich, is find out who that contact is and eliminate him in such a way that no suspicions are aroused over here. A car crash, perhaps, or some form of accident in the home. I don't care how you do it as long as it doesn't spook the natives over here. Do you understand?'

'Yes. This man is a sympathiser?'

'Right up your alley, I'd say. The last thing anybody wants is someone like that in a position to help these people, wouldn't you agree?'

'I would.' Another pause. 'I will do this thing you ask because it is within the task I have taken upon myself. But know this: if you make a single move toward my family I will make finding you my task. I will hunt you—'

'Yeah, yeah: you'll hunt me down like a dog, or some other animal. I know the routine. Word of advice: don't. I'll play straight by you if you play straight by me, and if you come looking—'

'I too have heard it before.'

'Then we both know where we stand.'

'I believe so.'

'Good.'

'Oh shit.' Penny Marsh was still less than happy about things, and the news that we were leaving the country had done nothing for her mood. 'Now I've got to get the BfV on board and organise clearance to operate in Germany. Thanks a lot.'

'Don't worry, we're not going.'

'But you just said—'

'That the order had been given. I didn't say that it was going to be followed through. Trust me, there's no need to worry your opposite numbers in Germany.'

'Trust you.'

'I haven't steered you wrong yet, have I?'

'Not as far as I know, but that doesn't mean anything.'

'Penny, I've already put a plan of my own in place. We're not going to Germany. Well, we won't be going to Wewelsburg anyway.'

'And then what?'

'Then I'll improvise.'

'Improvise.'

'Yeah, improvise. You'd better get used to this if you want to stay in the field, Penny. Plans don't go the way you want, people don't act the way you want and the X-factor always gets in the way. If you're going to dance with the fuck-up fairy, you'd better learn to think on your feet – the bitch keeps changing steps.'

'Cut the crap, will you? I don't need another lecture from Mr Know-It-All, I need to know what's going on.'

'Right. Short version: the castle gets pulled, we have to pick a new spot, I make sure it stays in this country.'

'And then?'

'Nature takes its course.'

'I don't like it. Upstairs is pushing to roll this up now and I agree with them. We've got enough to arrest everyone in the group, publicly humiliate them and make sure that they never have a chance to do anything like this again. In fact, we've had it for months. The only reason this operation's still going on is because you say so, and I'm getting sick of begging for more time at every bloody debrief. I'm due in again next week, and this time I'm going to suggest finishing this once and for all.'

'No, you're not.'

'Why? I know you're not telling me everything, but this is getting silly. If you've got something going on then it's about time you gave me the bigger picture and stopped pissing about with the mind games. I'm bored of not being cleared, I'm bored of your mysterious bloody agency and I'm bored beyond all possible measure of being your bloody mushroom!'

'Because we're going to roll it up instead.'

'How the hell am I supposed to cover that up? It's one thing lying about you, but what am I supposed to say when your mob show up and arrest everyone?'

'That's not quite—'

'Oh, you're going to kill them? What makes you think you're going to be able to kill that many people with impunity? The real world doesn't work like that. Just because you can boss me around you think that the police will ignore it? The papers? With all the bigwigs running this thing there's no way you can expect to keep it quiet.'

'We have our ways.'

'I told you to skip the mysterious crap. Either you start explaining things to me or I start planning to roll this up.'

'I can't.'

'I'm not cleared for it.'

'No, you're not. And if you find out much more you're going to be in trouble. You're close enough to that point as it is.'

'Really.'

'Really. You know my face, you know that I work for people who can co-opt an entire MI5 operation with one simple statement and you've had more than enough chance to check my fingerprints and find that the records don't match anything like what you'd previously expected. You aren't even supposed to know that we exist, Penny, and unless you keep your head down someone back home is going to start paying attention to the fact that you do.'

'And then what?'

'You want a diagram?'

'Oh.'

'Yeah. We play for keeps, Penny.'

I hated having to threaten Penny like that. We'd been getting on and it felt like a shitty thing to do. The only reason I did was to stop her, though: I wasn't kidding about what was likely to happen if she kept asking questions. I was doing what I could to protect her from the Service's machinery, the measures we're prepared to take to remain secret. The Boss had ordered more powerful people than her dead, and once that order came down there was no place to hide and no way to stop it. I didn't want that to happen to her, and the only alternative was to piss her off again. It wasn't fair: I was getting away with this under her good offices and even though she didn't know it, she was saving her own people back home an awful lot of trouble. But I didn't think things would be any easier for her if she knew that, which is why I didn't bother telling her.

But if I had to be honest, underneath it all was an expectation that the Boss would decide that Penny knew too much and had to go, and my real hope that the old bastard wouldn't order *me* to do it.

Chapter Twenty-One

When you get past all the unpleasantness, I'm really just another civil servant. Like most of the rest, I hate my job, don't much like most of the people I work with and hope that all the bullshit will eventually turn into early retirement and a nice pension.

And I hate my Boss.

Imagine, then, my joy when I discovered that my next minicab ride had the evil old git as my driver. It was odd to see him outside the office, hunched over the wheel and swearing at the traffic like a pro. The England football shirt was a bit much, though – blending in is one thing, and it fitted visually, but somehow I just couldn't see him cheering the boys along down the pub on a Saturday afternoon. My image of the man was behind a desk, sending blokes like me off to do his dirty work in the morning and spending the afternoon in his club screwing with the rich and powerful, so this . . . well, even by my standards, this was just weird.

'A month, then.' Not one for small talk, the Boss. Not even a claim to have had that Aleister Crowley in the back of his cab once.

'Just over three weeks now, sir, and two until the equipment needs to be ready for transport to Germany.'

'I don't want them leaving the country. Makes things too complicated.'

'Already in hand, sir. I've got an outsider on it.'

'Von Oderbar?' The old man snorted. 'You'd have done better to eliminate him.'

'The circumstances might well do that for us, and if he's caught he won't have anything to tell beyond me putting him up to it. The Service is insulated.'

'Unless you start talking.'

'I don't think that's likely, sir.'

'Not an acceptable risk, and you know what happens if you become a liability.'

'I won't.'

'What about the Marsh woman, then? What have you told her?'

'Drugs and special effects, sir.'

'Good grief, do people still believe that?'

'It's easier to believe than the alternative, sir. She's holding MI5 off to give us room to move, so she must be buying at least some of it. Having her inside has made the job easier to run – the last thing we need is someone else poking their noses in.'

'Keep an eye on her. I'll want to review what she knows at the end of this before I decide her future.' I'd guessed that was coming, of course. What he meant was deciding whether or not she *had* a future.

'Sir.' I could hardly throw a fit in the back of the cab, but when the time came to report I planned to make a vigorous case in her defence. She'd been a good girl and would still be walking away from this with a feather in her cap. I had plans to make sure of that, and since she still didn't know anything of real value about me or the Service, there was no point killing someone who could be useful again.

'Sir, I'll want to put in for some leave after this is over.'

'We'll see about that afterwards, once we know how much of this mess is left to clear up.'

'Can't someone else take care of it?'

'Depends on what the situation is. If your cover's intact then we'll want to use the enemy's remaining trust in you to clear up any stragglers.'

'Right.' I didn't fancy the idea of running the foot soldiers to ground, but the Boss wasn't exactly sensitive to his employees' desires.

'So you'd better make sure you get the lot in one fell swoop.'

'What about Five? If it's just the plebs, surely we can leave them to deal with the mop-up?'

'Not until we know who knows what. We're not sharing this one – I want it all wrapped up internally. Keep me informed of developments, and make sure this stays inside the country. If we get them all together, and we do it on British soil, you'll be on leave this time next month.'

I was going to need that leave. I was getting to the point where things started to chafe – from Folkestone's chummy evil to Sir James's confidence in the rightness of his cause, but even sitting at a desk five days a week had lost any kind of interest for me. And it was starting to become an effort to maintain the cover. I had to carry on playing it right, though, since Michael was still there keeping an eye on me at work and I was still supposed to be tutoring the moron. I already knew what was going to happen to Michael after this was over, and that at least gave me some cheer. The virus was already sitting quietly on his computer at home and when the time came he'd suddenly have a history of professionally questionable communications going back years that would put him right in the frame for insider trading. From there he would head into the justice system and somehow be routed to the kind of prison they don't usually put rich kids in. After that I gave him a fortnight, tops, before he found himself shivved while no one was looking.

All that, and the chance to be treated the same way he'd treated the ladies of our back office. He'd make someone a lovely wife, inside.

My exfiltration was due to happen just before Michael's, and was nice and simple: I was going to be recalled to the Army as a reservist and sent to Afghanistan. Given how bad a hash our leaders had made of the thing, nobody would be surprised to see me go. I was hoping to time it so that Michael would be picked up while everyone was distracted by my departure, just to see it wrapped up nice and neatly. It was worth a shot, anyway.

I spent the next ten days keeping my head down while I started pulling together the various things we'd need in Germany. Mostly it was just a matter of being in a particular place to receive a delivery, and most of those were fairly small packages that were easy enough to transfer in public places. I carried a lot of brief-cases and manbags, picked up a couple of vans and rode in more taxis than I wanted to remember. Nothing about this gig had been easy so far, and this bit continued the 'let's fuck with Jack's head' theme when I got to spend a Saturday afternoon receiving a twenty-foot shipping container at our main storage facility. Normally there was no way anyone from outside would have been allowed to know the location, but the delivery man was an extremely trustworthy one.

As well as a mate.

'What the hell are you doing here, Hamlet?' Brutus was six and a half feet of solid muscle, black as a lawyer's heart and one of the more entertaining people in the subculture that dealt with weird shit. He's got a thing for Shakespeare, and another for confidentiality, which led to him naming me after 'the most miserable motherfucker he ever saw'. I can't fault his logic – the man's an information broker and knows he can't sell me out if he hasn't got the data. It might not sound like much, but between an ex-Man in Black like him and a spooky spook like me that's a pretty big deal.

'I'm working.'

'These are bad people, man. You OK?'

'As ever.'

'That bad, huh?'

'Not yet, but it will be in a couple of weeks.'

'Well, I won't be crying 'bout it. These crackers pay well, but their . . . proclivities aren't really my thing. Must have bust their balls to do business with a black man.'

'At least you're straight.'

'Says who?' Brutus grinned and I chuckled.

'Don't ask, right?'

'And don't tell.'

What Brutus had brought to me didn't seem to be on my inventory. I'd been called away from an afternoon with Penny, working the couple thing, to come in and accept it because Sir James was in Derbyshire for the weekend. I had the feeling that the association with Brutus wasn't something he wanted generally known, but whether that was because of his colour or for some deeper reason I had no idea. The container itself matched the one I already had half-loaded with torches, robes, incense and a thousand other bits of paraphernalia, which presumably meant that I was now going to have to find a second truck to get it across France. A little more warning would have been nice, since even though I knew we wouldn't be taking the trip I still had to make it look as if I thought we were. It was also sealed, so there was no chance of a sneak peek at the contents. My only clue was the refrigeration unit plugged into one end and the fact that it was only slightly colder than ambient to the touch, which suggested a pretty big chunk of insulation inside. Whatever this thing held, then, was either perishable or unstable at room temperature. I couldn't decide which was worse.

*

That Monday, I met the reason for Sir James's absence: Henry George Arthur Williams, his lordship's grandson and, thanks to my efforts, primary heir. The boy was tall, blond and good-looking, the perfect blueprint for an Aryan poster boy, right down to the palpable air of superiority. It never ceases to amuse me that pretty much the entire leadership of outfits like this one fell ludicrously short of the ideal – Himmler, a short, fat, four-eyed git, would never have got into the SS he led, for example – but for once they had really got it right.

'Mr Dennis, it's a pleasure to finally meet you.' His eyes were piercing – a cold blue that would fix an ordinary man like a specimen on a microscope slide and see straight through him. There was intelligence in there, too, and no small measure of cruelty.

'Thank you, sir. It's an honour.'

'I understand from Sir James that you've been extremely helpful to us over the last year.'

'I've certainly tried to be, sir.' It was obvious that he liked the 'sir', and expected the deference. Playing it like a soldier seemed the way to go – treat the bastard like a visiting bigwig and hope he went away happy.

'The way you dealt with the obstacle that my father represented was quite inspired. If I hadn't known that the operation was planned I would never have suspected a thing.'

'You're too kind, sir. I couldn't have done it without—'

'Without Folkestone? Of course. He's such an interesting fellow, isn't he? Such a rare gift he has.'

'Indeed so, sir.' That was certainly one way of putting it.

'Yes, indeed so. He's been kind enough to teach me a little of his art – fascinating stuff. My father had to go, of course – the man was a disgrace. If he'd been allowed to inherit my grandfather's legacy there would have been no end of trouble. Silly bastard couldn't keep his trousers up for a start, and then there was the money: he'd have blown the lot on cars and women before we could have stopped him. At least he died doing something he loved, and isn't that how we'd all like to go?'

'I should think so, sir, yes.' His grandfather's legacy was one thing, but the boy was showing his great-grandfather's legacy even more. To stand there talking so coolly with his father's killer took a particular type of coldness, one that I was sure the Eagle Society had been carefully nurturing throughout his life.

'Are you looking forward to Germany?'

'Very much so, sir. I hear it's beautiful at this time of year.'

'Not a patch on what's to come though, eh? Getting things back as they're supposed to be and so on.'

Sir James had been talking to someone else while I'd been distracting the boy, and chose this point to re-enter the conversation. 'I hope John's been keeping you entertained, Henry. He's quite a fellow, and no small asset to our cause.'

'He has, James, yes.' No need for 'sir' from this young man, apparently. 'Aren't we supposed to be picking up my uniform now, though?'

'We are, Henry, and we should let John get on with the arrangements. Would you give us a moment?'

'Of course.' The boy nodded, more in dismissal than anything else, and headed to the car.

'Is everything all right, Sir James?'

'It is. Very much so, in fact. The gentleman I've just been speaking to while you were with young Henry will be ensuring that the containers aren't delayed en route to the staging point. The vehicles will be here on Sunday to collect them.'

'But I've already arranged—'

'Change of plan. We've decided to use people from another group with similar goals to our own. We're part of a bigger project, John, and if the other players are able to help us, it makes sense to let them rather than risk using outsiders.'

'What about security? If they know about us—'

'They won't. All they'll do is what they're told. No questions, no argument. These Eastern Europeans are very good at that. They won't know what they're carrying and you're to make sure that everything is secured before their arrival. Is everything running to schedule?'

'Spot on, Sir James. We'll be locked down and ready to move by Saturday lunchtime.'

'Good man.'

I let him go as quickly as I could, since I had another fish to fry. While I'd been talking to the new Führer, I'd also been keeping an eye on Sir James and his friend – and that friend had been worrying me. His photograph had cropped up in the background information I'd read over a year before with a note that he wasn't any kind of concern to us. Not something I'd generally think twice about, but when the file says a man's dead, it's normally right. After all, we have ways of making sure; calling someone back to check the story isn't likely to cause the Boss too many headaches and we've got people who are more than capable of doing so. When one of *our* files says a man's dead, it's not like another agency guessing. We usually *know.*

This did not bode well.

Chapter Twenty-Two

Things progressed according to plan for the rest of the week. I had everything organised by Friday night, with only the final lock-down to take care of on Saturday afternoon before the trucks came to collect their cargo on Sunday. As far as the Eagle Society was concerned, things were perfect.

Which was exactly the way things weren't supposed to be.

I'd not heard a peep out of Heinrich since I'd given him his orders to take out the bent curator, and was starting to worry that he might have decided to double-cross me. At least I could be reasonably sure that he'd not told the authorities, since that was something I would have heard about one way or the other – either from the Boss, or from Folkestone as he came to drag me away for some of his very particular sport. But inaction in this case was just as bad when it came to throwing the necessary spanner in the works. Letting the group out of the country would cause a pile of jurisdictional nightmares in this case: the Germans are understandably touchy when it comes to certain matters, and I don't blame them for it at all. Sending a team of our own into Wewelsburg was the sort of thing the Germans would be likely to notice, and I didn't fancy having to get myself out of a mess like that. Better to keep this little problem at home, and deal with it quietly.

I thought about it for a while and realised that I still had a couple of options. They weren't great, but they could be made to do in a pinch and since this was about to become one I was willing to consider risking the fallout.

Then again, perhaps telling all to Penny wasn't the best idea I've ever had.

'I don't like it.'

'Neither do I, hence the fallback plan.'

'What about sabotaging the trucks?'

'They come in, they load, they go. Shouldn't take more than half an hour, and I won't have time.'

'I could do it.'

'No way. If they see you we're both dead.'

'Then what about calling your people?'

'I haven't exactly had the opportunity.'

'Except that you could have left early and done it then.' She almost had a point there. I'd spent the night on her sofa after a very nice dinner at a little place in Chelsea – we'd decided it was time we started sleeping together.

'If you think we're not being watched constantly you're a lot more naive than I gave you credit for, Penny. Plus, I wouldn't have been able to brief you. You're the one who goes on about being kept in the loop.'

'Then I could call my people.'

'That would violate security.'

'So would the transfer to Germany.'

'So I'll claim that there's something wrong with one of the containers, and force them to be recalled.'

'Such as?'

'I'm working on it.'

'Great, the genius at work.'

'Something like that, yeah.'

'And what if you don't persuade them to bring the containers back?'

'I'll improvise. I'm pretty good at this, Penny. You just need to trust me a little bit longer.'

'The circumstances aren't helping.'

'Don't worry about it, seriously. We're rolling this up a week from today no matter what, and I want it to be as easy as possible. That means staying here, so I'll find a way.' I had an idea – a messy idea, but an idea nonetheless – but it was going to make me about as popular as Milli Vanilli at an acoustic night if I had to use it. Nothing like a heroic last move to get the blood racing, though, and you need to keep your sense of humour at times like this. 'Tell you what: I bet you dinner once all this is over that we'll wrap this bastard in England. Deal?' That earned me an arched eyebrow.

'You'll bet me dinner? Is that really an appropriate reaction to all this?'

'If you can't take a joke, you shouldn't have joined.'

I was still working out exactly how this plan of mine was going to pan out when I got to the warehouse. My options were running out fast and so was time. When the trucks pulled in I was pretty sure I could make it work without exposing myself. I calculated cut-outs and blinds while I watched the drivers lowering the containers into position on their trailers, checked the seals as I memorised number plates and watched them leave to the sudden realisation that the Eagle Society probably had a mole to prevent anything stopping those trucks. That left only the last-ditch Hail Mary play. The one that would probably end my career and could end up causing more grief for the Service than any other individual had managed in twenty years.

But I had orders and, more importantly, there was a bet on it.

The trucks were scheduled to stop overnight just outside Dover and board the ferry early the next morning. This was to make sure that both sets of drivers were fresh enough to make the run with as few stops as possible, and to let them skip the tourist traffic. It was a good plan, allowing them to slide unnoticed among the other HGVs and pass without comment – plain sight is frequently the best place to hide a vehicle on the move. All nice and smooth, simple, easy and effective.

So I'd do the deed that night, once I'd reported in to Sir James, so it would all be in play by the morning.

Sir James was delighted to hear that everything had gone to plan. 'Well done, John: an excellent piece of work. Now I need you to fly out in the morning to meet the trucks when they arrive on Monday.'

'Tuesday, surely.'

'Change of plan. The trucks are going non-stop, switching drivers en route. The layovers were thought to be too dangerous.'

'So they're already out of the country?'

'Off the boat and on the *Autoroute*, according to the schedule.'

'So why have me put the plan together?'

'As a blind. We don't want Customs getting in the way, and if the freelancers you booked let anything slip we'd have to eliminate them. This way they know a schedule, and if anyone does ask questions there's a layer of disinformation in place to throw them off the scent.'

'What about the staging point?'

'A false address. Anyone searching there will find an ecclesiastical supplier, and can spend a week or two testing communion wafers if that's what amuses them. Meanwhile our shipment will arrive at the real staging point in plenty of time for you to prepare everything for a fast transfer to the castle on Saturday afternoon.'

'Right. So what should I tell Miss Gentle? She's expecting to spend the day with me tomorrow.'

'That you are needed, and that the two of you can have some

time together when all this is over. In fact, I have a villa in Tuscany you can borrow if you like. It's not the ideal season, I admit, but my wife tells me that it's very romantic all the same. When are you planning to pop the question?'

'Pop the . . . Oh, not for a while yet. We both want to be sure.'

'Very sensible. If only more people did that we'd have a much more stable society. You won't be moving in together until you do, though, will you? We do tend to frown on that sort of thing.'

'As do I, Sir James. We won't be moving in together any time soon.'

I'd barely got to bed when the phone rang. Sir James's voice sounded worried.

'John, I want you to meet me at the warehouse.'

'When?'

'Now. We have a problem.' I kept my breathing steady even as my heart was doing backflips. 'Our contact at the castle has just been arrested.'

'What happened?'

'It would appear that he'd been sleeping with his boss's wife, and was discovered *in flagrante delicto* last night. There was a struggle.'

'Oh no. How bad?'

'He killed the husband.'

'Shit. Can't we bail him out?'

'Not without tipping our hand. His wife is leaving him in jail – we've lost our access.'

'That's bloody unlucky timing.'

'Yes, it is. I'd like to know why the husband chose this particular night to come home early, but he's not really in a position to tell.' I was willing to bet a certain German had something to do with it. Heinrich had played a blinder there, and as long as he stayed out of the rest of this, I was willing to leave him alone as a reward.

'Can't we pull him back?'

'No, John. Not on such short notice. It takes a lot of arrangements to do that sort of thing and we haven't even got any of his possessions to use as a focus.'

'I could fly out there and—'

'No. We'll need to relocate the ritual.'

'What's wrong with waiting?' I was curious about this. They'd been playing a long game for more than fifty years and there had to be a reason for the sudden rush.

'There's a particular stellar alignment that we've discovered can work to our advantage in retrieving the Führer. Given the difficulty we had with all of us working together and the problems of recruiting replacements for the circle, this is our best chance of success before Lord Williams dies – and I'd much rather the Führer had time to acclimatise himself before any publicity started, wouldn't you?'

'Of course. So what's the plan?'

'I've already recalled the trucks – they'll be here early tomorrow morning. You and I are going to scout alternative locations while the others are out of the country. It's too late for them to change their business plans without arousing suspicion.'

'What about my plans?'

'You'll still be out of the country as far as the bank is concerned, and I'm quite sure you'll bring the client on board no matter where you are. I need a calm head for this, John. Are you up to it?'

'Absolutely.'

'Good man. Let's get moving.'

The late-night roads were clear and we shot out of London at high speed. Sir James turned out to be quite a driver, throwing his Jaguar around the road like an old-school bank robber, and by the time dawn broke we were in the West Country. The day passed in a blur of old stone circles and places with tenuous links to everyone from King Arthur to the last of the mythical witch-kings. It made sense that we were going for the more obscure sites – the last thing we needed was anyone coming upon us by accident. We spent the night in an old pub, and worked up as far as Birmingham the next day. Wales was eliminated for not being England, which saved us an awful lot of time, and by Wednesday evening we'd covered almost every likely site in the southern half of the country. It did, at least, give us what looked like the right spot for our revised plans to take shape – but I didn't get a chance to talk to Penny. My hope was that she'd kept her head and done as she was told, and had by now been informed by the Society itself that there was a change of plan. Her position should have got her that information ahead of the plebs, at least, and thus would her patience have been rewarded with the promised result: the chance to buy me dinner.

The Thursday brought me back to London, to check over the containers and arrange their despatch to the new ritual site. It might have been a pain in the arse for me, but it also gave me hope. The Eagle Society was sufficiently arrogant to believe that nothing could stand in its way, which would make a strike from within both easier and more effective when the time came. I'd made my own personal preparations for what was to come, and had also ensured that the Boss had all the information he'd need to get my backup in place and ready for the magic moment.

But there was the pain to deal with first. Bart was my shipping contact, a nasty little man who'd happily move anything any-where as long as the price was right. I personally wouldn't have used him to bring my shopping back from the supermarket, but I'd been told to keep things in the family and he was a known fellow traveller. Something about his grandfather having been mixed up with getting people out of trouble after the war, apparently, and that had led to the family business. Bart's kid, Johann, was smarter, and would do good things with the company when his father got out of the way, but for now I had to deal with the slimeball.

'Of course, I would very much like to help you. But such a thing is just not possible at such short notice.' He had the whine in his voice already, even before I'd started applying pressure. How a man could whine in baritone was beyond me, but Bart managed it somehow. 'There are arrangements to make, preparing the drivers and their vehicles, and the paperwork – that has to be organised also.'

'You told me last week that you could arrange this in a day.'

'Last week, yes. But things change, and now I do not have the staff available to facilitate this. You understand, of course.'

'I understand that you're screwing me around, Bart.'

'No, that is not what I am doing. I am sharing the facts with you, and allowing you to see why this thing cannot be done. I could simply have told you "no" over the telephone.'

'No you wouldn't. You've got more sense than to make me come looking for you.'

'I could arrange for this to happen on Saturday afternoon, but not before. Even then it will be difficult, but I will rearrange things so you have your drivers. The vehicles, of course, are here already.' That was true – we'd made sure that the containers stayed on their trailers, so all that Bart was messing me around on was the tractor units and men to drive them.

'That won't do. My employer needs the cargo in place on Saturday morning.'

'This is most irregular. I do not wish to be the masked knocker, but your employer has not organised this very well at all.'

'The masked what?'

'Masked knocker. You know, one who criticises from behind. You do not know the phrase?' He looked surprised at this.

'No, Bart, because it's bollocks. Like everything else you're telling me. Now do I get the trucks or not?'

'Trucks, yes. But not drivers. I will not have anyone available until—'

'Friday night, when the load needs to move.' I pulled a pistol from under my jacket and started fitting a suppressor.

'It cannot be done!' The rising tone of his voice was satisfying and his eyes, which had barely met mine during three separate meetings, were now very firmly locked on what my hands were doing. 'If you had given me adequate notice it would be a different story!'

'Well, Bart, there are two ways we can go from here: either you tell me that everything will happen the way I want it, or Johann does when he inherits the business. Your choice.' I was a little surprised at how much this was affecting him, to be honest. I would have expected an obnoxious little shit like him to have been threatened often enough to get used to it.

'I'll try!'

'Trying isn't good enough, Bart. Just do as you're told and make the delivery.'

'But I'll have to cancel other jobs, break my word to other clients—'

'You've already broken your word to this one. Now I'm helping you put it right.'

'And what if they are angry? I might lose their custom. Will I be compensated?'

'Oh yes.' I smiled and pointed the gun at his left eye. 'Every breath you take from now on will be compensation.' Talk about cheesy lines, but Bart didn't deserve anything more original. 'Make the fucking call, Bart.'

'Not now. I must wait for the proper time.'

'Which is when?'

'From now, tomorrow morning.'

'Too late. Fix the trucks now and tell the client tomorrow.'

'No no no. That is not the way it works. Things must be done in their proper sequence.'

'Make the call, or I shoot you.'

'But it is not—' I squeezed the trigger, and Bart shut up. I was sick of him anyway.

Bart's phone was in his pocket, and Johann's number was easy enough to find. He answered on the second ring.

'Ja?'

'Your father just had a terrible accident. I need two trailers moved tomorrow night from London to Cambridgeshire, and I need you to arrange it immediately.'

'My father will have told you that it is not possible, yes?'

'Yes, he did, just before his accident.'

'That is not good, Mr Dennis. I have all the details of your meeting here, so I am quite aware of who you are.'

'That must be very reassuring for you. Now are you going to make your first business decision a good one, or do I have to come and discuss it with you in person?'

'I shall make the arrangements. But if we speak again, Mr Dennis, the conversation will not be so friendly.'

'You'll hunt me down and do nasty things to me, I'm sure. Not a wise idea, Johann, but I understand you might feel like you have to do something. Do this job and you'll never hear of me again. Deal?'

'I suppose, yes. Deal.'

Life is so much more civilised when people listen to reason.

There was still no word from Penny Marsh, though. Her mobile phone was switched off and there was no answer from her home number, so I was starting to fear the worst. Had she been pulled back in to Thames House, or had she screwed up somehow? If it was the latter, there was a real chance that the whole operation could be ruined at the last minute, and that would never have done. I made a note of that in my report, along with details of container movements and the new location for Saturday night's ritual. Everything I could think of went into that report . . .

Because there was an increasing likelihood that it was going to be my last.

Chapter Twenty-Three

'We have something of a problem, John. Miss Gentle appears to have been serving another master.' Sir James's matter-of-fact tone really didn't do much for my confidence. 'You didn't mention anything you shouldn't have to her, did you? Pillow talk and so on?'

'Good God, no.' I was doing a pretty good impression of being horrified, mainly because I was genuinely upset. Having seen what happened to people who crossed the Society, my hopes for her safety were somewhat low. 'Did you at least stop her from reporting in?'

'Folkestone picked her up while you and I were scouting locations. She was on her way to meet a contact then. Fortunately, our man on the inside was able to let us know when and where her meeting was, so she didn't make it.'

'What was she, Special Branch?'

'MI5. Our man was able to stall her operation, but hasn't got to her reports yet. I'll be interested to see what she had to say about us.'

'Where is she now?'

'One of Folkestone's people is looking after her for the moment. We thought you might like to be involved in the interrogation.'

'Very much. How badly exposed are we?'

'Nowhere near as badly as you might think. Her handler's

been taken care of with a bout of food poisoning, and by Monday there won't be anything anyone can do to stop us. We'll have the whole thing buried in a week. No one's going to miss Miss Gentle.'

'Does this affect the timetable?'

'Not at all. You and Folkestone can start work on her after the weekend – she's not important enough to interrupt anything for.'

So they'd had Penny for at least three days. It was Saturday morning, ten hours before the ritual, and we were supervising the construction of the ritual space. We'd brought our own circle this time, and were loading it into the remains of a druidic grove in Cambridgeshire. After all the switching around that had been pulled up to now, I was surprised by the fact that it was the one we'd picked out.

Around us, the foot soldiers were hard at work setting up wooden pillars, torches and banners. A new altar had been built, and a chair placed before it that looked like something out of an old horror movie – the sort of thing you'd expect to find a certain well-known Carpathian nobleman sitting in. Beyond them, a loose ring of armed men made sure that we weren't going to be disturbed. It was like some weird hybrid of movie set, cult headquarters and Army post – one that I really didn't like at all.

I moved outside to join Folkestone, who was positioning the outer ring of guards who'd be our first line of defence if anyone came calling. Despite Sir James's confidence in his people at MI5, we were obviously not taking any chances.

'Sorry about your girlfriend, sir.' He sounded genuinely regretful, too. 'We all thought you had a good thing going on there.' A couple of the foot soldiers within hearing distance nodded in agreement.

'So did I, Folkestone. But we'll worry about it on Monday.' There was no time for me to be concerned about Penny, either as a loyal member of the Eagle Society or as myself. Folkestone seemed to take it as a sign of stoicism – a man of action focusing on one job at a time. It appeared to impress the boys, too: as we walked away I heard comments pass between them about what a hard bastard I was and how my dedication was approved of.

'Do you want to be in on the interrogation, sir? I can understand if you'd rather not.'

'Not at all, Folkestone. After the bitch played me like that, the least I can do is return the favour. We'll empty that pretty head of hers, then start explaining the error of her ways.'

'As you say, sir. Now, about the guards . . .'

We took a walk around the perimeter. Folkestone's positioning was good, and there was nothing I could do to make the strike team's job easier without arousing suspicion. The Service guys are good, though, so I was expecting them to get through even if they had to fight to do it.

The sun came down as we finalised our preparations. Each of us was in our black uniform, except for the Williams boy, who wore the brown favoured by Hitler in life. I was sure that he thought it auspicious, but I suspected it was more likely intended to make the once and future Führer feel more at home in his new body from the start. Knives, torches, cups and wands were ready, and I had a little something of my own to back up the pistol that was part of my uniform. The spare magazine in my tunic pocket wasn't exactly regulation, either, but I was rather hoping it wouldn't be necessary.

A horn sounded, then another joined it, then a third and a fourth. The note was mournful, like a hunting call caught on the wind and brought to us from another place entirely. The wind picked up a little, but that was probably just the weather joining in for the sake of atmosphere rather than any magical effect. We'd only just started, after all.

We approached differently this time from the last when everything had gone wrong. Each of us had a starting position of our own, two to each point of the compass. The lines we'd been given were split between each pair so that the quarters were called by both rather than having a single spokesman per direction. It was an interesting technical move, and one that I figured had something to do with avoiding any unfortunate surprises. There were thirteen steps to be taken before we reached the ring of draped banners that prevented us from seeing into the circle itself, one for each member of the original group. Sir James was already in there as we walked – I could hear him chanting in a language that sounded slightly familiar, each word grating on my aura as he forced them through a throat not designed for noises like that. The tone of his voice had a quality of wrongness to it, a timbre that teetered on the edge of reason and made me wonder exactly what I was about to walk into. I wouldn't have minded knowing more, but to follow the words too closely would have dragged me into them and possibly outside my safety zone. It was a choice between that and maintaining my shields so I could keep thinking straight and level – really not what I'd call a difficult decision. By the time we were halfway to the drapes I could hear four new voices rising to join with Sir James's chanting, and where his had been disturbing, these were immediately starting to form into a little knot of madness and panic in the back of my brain. I glanced to my left and saw Thomas, my partner in the South, starting to glaze over a little. His right hand was trembling visibly even though his steps were solid, and I wondered how much faith he was running on – and in what.

Three steps away from the curtain, and I felt as if my head was going to explode. Whatever Sir James had organised was ten times more powerful than I'd thought him capable of, and I started to take the possibility of the ritual's success much more seriously. I'd tooled up more from habit than anything else, since I don't like being caught unprepared. Was I ever thanking that habit now.

Passing through the curtain . . .

If I hadn't been so focused on holding my shields together, the transition into the circle might well have unhinged me completely. The energy was ferocious already, before we'd even begun the full working. My head felt close to bursting just from the Hellish maelstrom that Sir James had summoned. Then I saw them.

He'd had help. At each of the four quarters stood a dead man, the four men who'd previously been members of our circle. They were chanting in unison, their voices keen with the awful power that was still trying to claw away at my shields and rip through my sanity. Their arms were raised towards the sky, heads tilted back and, just to really trip a man over the edge into madness, the bastards were on fire. The smell was doing to my stomach what the noise was trying to do to my mind, and it took an effort not to lose my lunch all over the floor.

The other seven men who'd entered with me had quite clearly lost any grip they might once have held on reality. They were each robotically singing their own parts of the melody, the parts we'd each been given as a chant for calling the quarters. I sang my own, then, to be sure of fitting in, and rocked my torso in the same little circle as the others. The sensory overload was incredible: incense mixed with burning flesh and the assault on my ears to make remembering the words I was supposed to be chanting difficult. Mist was forming along the ground again, like the last time we'd tried this but thicker. And then, from the west, came the boy.

The ritual was having an effect all right. The boy who would be Führer strode through the mist towards the altar and its chair as though he were already the master of the world. It was as if he crackled with an electricity of his own, pulling the mist around him with each step, calling it to him. By the time he reached the chair most of the mist had gone, a faint residue visible only in the shape of his footprints, and as he sat the last of it flowed up into his hands.

I had to hold on, despite the pull of what was happening around me. Looking up, I could see clouds forming over the circle, mirroring what had happened before with the mist. With each repeat of the chant, they seemed to be getting lower.

Time had given up any relevance not long after we entered the circle. We chanted over and over, rocking our bodies while the corpses sang. Somewhere in all the noise I could hear Sir James screaming Hitler's name along with those of several demons, calling the former forward even as he bound the latter to stand still and let him. It was one hell of a piece of magic, to be honest.

The clouds had sunk again while I'd been looking elsewhere, and now they formed a roof that sealed us off from our last reminder of reality. I wasn't even sure if we were in the same place where we'd started or had hopped across dimensions as a result of the ritual. The fog started flowing out from underneath the chair as Henry spread his hands open in front of him, palms down. The clouds above and below matched perfectly in colour and motion, a funnel leaving the centre of each to stretch out and touch the other in a column of smoke and fire. All around us the air churned with power, perspective and depth perception flickering from one extreme to the other. One moment the circle was impossibly small, the next a thousand miles across. I could feel my shields starting to weaken under the assault.

At some unseen signal, the four dead men took a pace forward, towards the centre. That was Henry's cue to act. He left his seat slowly, stepping towards the central column. With each step he took, the column moved faster. I could hear screaming, and had to check that it wasn't me. The gateway was opening again.

The column exploded into white fire as Henry Williams entered, his arms held wide, ready to accept the blessing of his ancestor. At the last moment, I was sure I could see his eyes widen with understanding – a sudden realisation of how he'd been used and betrayed – before they went dead as his soul was sucked out.

Then silence, for a second that lasted for ever.

The column changed, then. White light became pure darkness, hiding the vacant body from sight. The dead men moved forward again, still singing as they burned, moving towards the column as one. I was starting to lose it. I could feel my mind slipping away slowly, pulled in by the horror of what I was seeing and doing. My nose felt as if it was bleeding, my movements weren't quite my own any more and my voice was getting more hoarse. How much longer would I be able to hold out, and would it be long enough?

When the four dead men met at the pillar, I had my answer. There was an explosion of silence, a sudden stillness that left me reeling for a moment as my eyes and balance tried to grasp the laws of normality taking grip once more. Everything suddenly stopped.

There was a strange popping noise in the distance that took me a moment to identify: gunfire.

In the centre of the circle, Sir James and the young man in brown were looking at each other. Sir James's face was full of adoration, Henry's empty. Then, as though waking from a dream, the boy opened his mouth.

And Adolf Hitler screamed.

It was a worse sound than the ritual that had summoned him: the sound of a man after more than fifty years in Hell. He frothed a little each time he drew breath, and the look in his eyes spoke of horrors I didn't even want to think about trying to guess at.

He was still screaming when I reached into my pocket, as I walked across to him, as I raised my arm in salute, and as I flicked out the blade of Vincent Alexander's cut-throat razor.

I'd been planning on having a smart line ready for this moment. Something clever that I could talk about at parties. But what do you say to Hitler when you look him in the face?

Nothing.

I brought the razor down fast, opening his throat from my right to left, curling with the cut to give me momentum to come back and punch Sir James right on the jaw. He went down like a sack of potatoes on top of the rapidly expiring Führer.

Everyone else in the circle was already down, bleeding from a selection of orifices and whimpering in pain. My knife was strapped on under the uniform, so putting them out of commission was quick and easy.

The gunfire was getting closer, and more frequent. Judging by the shouts from voices I recognised, Folkestone was running a good defence out there. That was going to get my people killed, so I needed to give them a little help. I burst out of the circle, rolling as I hit the ground and coming up into a crouch. There was my objective – ten yards away, using the cover to rest between shots.

'Folkestone! We need you!' He looked across to me, torn between duty to his men and duty to his leaders. Thank God for the *Führerprinzip*, since he gave a last quick order to his men – hold the position – and scuttled over to me.

'What's wrong?'

'Casualties inside, including the principal.'

'Shit!' Folkestone was moving fast, and beat me back through the draped banners by an easy second. He was gawping at the carnage when I came through.

'What the fuck happened?'

My answer to that was a punch to his solar plexus, which

would have been great if he hadn't blocked it. His fist hit me in the face like a jackhammer, and I suddenly realised the idiocy of going for someone with his kind of reflexes when I'd just narrowly avoided having my brains scooped out. My best option was to use the knife, but I wanted him alive so I could get Penny back. Not an optimal arrangement, since I was sure he didn't have any such worries.

I pulled out the gun again. Maybe if I just kneecapped him . . .

Not a chance. He knocked the gun out of my hand to the left, then sent me off to the right, a lovely little combination that put me flat on my arse. I must have been shagged if I let him get away with that one.

The knife, then. There was no way I could take him bare-handed, so I'd just have to go for minimum damage and slow him down to my level. I rolled over the ground towards him, catching the foot he was aiming for my head and sliding the knife across the back of his calf. Blood, a scream, and a textbook hamstringing. Down he went.

Right next to my bloody gun. This was not my day.

Few things in life are as embarrassing as being held at the point of your own weapon. If the strike team found me like this I'd never hear the end of it, and it wasn't that long since I'd finally got them to trust me with a weapon on one of their jobs. Something like this would be a running gag for the rest of my career.

'Give it up, Folkestone. Just tell me where the woman is.'

'Fuck you.' Why wasn't he firing?

'We'll cut you a deal.'

'How about I cut you one?'

'Go on.'

'Only two people know where she is, and the other one's with her.'

'Keep talking.' He obviously had a move in mind. All I had to do was spot it.

'If he doesn't hear from me by the morning, he'll go to work on her. He'll make it last, too. She'll be dying for days.'

'So how do we sort this out, Folkestone?'

'We don't.' He grinned, lifted the gun, and blew his own head off before I could stop him. He must have twigged that he wasn't coming out of this alive, so made sure that he got me one last time before he quit the field. You had to admire his nerve.

I was still looking at his body when the Boss appeared. A couple of guys from the strike team were loading Sir James onto a stretcher as he approached me.

'Get him?'

'Got him.' I pointed at the boy's body on the floor.

'Good.' He held out his hand for the razor, and I was happy to give it back. A nasty thing, that – old Vincent must have been some very special kind of bastard. 'Now go home.'

'What about Marsh?'

'She's dead, as far as we can tell. MI5 have her listed as killed on Wednesday, while you were in the country.'

'She was picked up by the Society.'

'Then bring her in for debriefing.'

I had an idea, but it needed to be played through quickly. The strike team were loading up into the helicopters that had arrived while the Boss and I were talking, and that was exactly what I needed.

'Drop me in London?'

'S'pose so. Northolt do you?'

'Perfect.'

I commandeered a car at RAF Northolt and drove hell-for-leather back to Penny's flat. Someone must have got their act together for a change, since I had a police escort after the second time they stopped me. RAF cars are not, on the whole, driven like that by people in blood-spattered SS uniforms, so the escort saved me a lot of questions when we shot through the West End at something not overly shy of sixty.

Penny wasn't in her flat, but what I needed was: her toothbrush and a comb with some of her hair caught in it. Plenty of her essence in both for me to get a trace.

Just a matter of relaxing, and letting her lead me to my target. Starting with the big front page of the street map, then localising it down again and again. I could have killed for better maps, but time was something of a factor. Then my brain started working and I downloaded maps from the Internet. The whole thing took something like an hour and a half, but at the end of it I knew where to find her.

The cheeky fuckers had her stashed in the same building I'd used for storing the containers.

I still had a key for that.

'We're moving.' The guard wasn't expecting me, and certainly not in uniform. The blood probably surprised him a bit as well, but not as much as the knife in his throat. Half a dozen men in black jumpsuits fanned out behind me as I walked across the floor to the office section, covering all the angles like the professionals they were. Through the door and into the office I'd been using – no sign of life. Likewise the next office, and the one after that. I sent four men upstairs to check there, but again there was nothing. We started shifting cabinets, tables, anything big enough to hide a trapdoor – and still there was nothing. I started swearing and kicked the wall. That actually made me feel better, so I did it again. The fourth kick hit a hollow section of wall.

'Find the mechanism.'

I'm pretty good, but six members of our strike team leave me far behind. Within a minute I was through the secret door and walking up to the mysterious man that Folkestone had trusted with Penny's death.

'Hello, Martin,' I said, and shot him in the face.

Penny was in the far corner, tied, gagged and blindfolded. I let her loose to check out how she was. The way she held it together honestly impressed the hell out of me – she was all business.

'What happens now?'

'Debrief.'

'Are you going to take me in?'

'No. They are.' And the bag went over her head before she had time to work out who 'they' were.

Coda

'You're a cunt, Jack. You know that, right?'

'Yep.'

'You handed her over just like that?'

'What were my alternatives?'

'Arguing.'

'With the Boss? Do me a favour, Geoff. You know better than to fuck with the old man.'

I was on my third day of drinking, trying to get the sound of singing dead men out of my mind and finally starting to meet with some success. It had been too long since I'd seen real friends, which is why I was in Kensal Green, but the conversation wasn't going the way I'd hoped. Geoff and Sophie turned out to have some very firm opinions about how I'd left Penny Marsh.

'It's just a debrief.'

'Yeah. And then what?'

'Whatever the old bastard decides.'

'Care to hazard a guess?'

'The usual.' Yes, all right, there was more than one reason I was drinking. I wasn't exactly proud of letting them cart Penny off with a chloroformed bag over her head, but I hadn't exactly been awash with alternatives. My guitar playing had been off since I got back, too, and that was a really bad sign. I can usually play through the blues and find my way back from there, but I was having real trouble letting go of this one. After all, Penny was officially already dead.

'Come on, Sophie, surely you can see that I was stuffed.'

'I can see that you're a shit.'

'Thanks.'

'What did you expect me to say?'

'How about that I didn't put her there? MI5 sent her in, and MI5 got her caught. At least this way she gets it quickly.'

'Well, that's nice.'

'Ever seen someone tortured to death, Sophie? Geoff has, haven't you, mate?' Geoff had the good sense not to answer that. 'A week to die, and all of it in pain. That would make what happened to you look like a trip to the fucking spa.'

'Nicely put.' Sophie walked off.

'Look, mate, you've got to at least try to do something about it.'

'Such as? It's not like we ever get a lot of input in the decision-making process, is it?'

'Talk to the Boss. See if he'll listen to reason. Try to get her something.'

'All that's going to do is make him think I've gone soft.'

'Haven't you?'

'Not yet. There's a few more years left in me.'

'Then why are you sitting here pissed at four in the morning?'

'I thought you might like some company.'

'Right. Piss off home, Jack, and come back when you've got your shit together. You're just embarrassing yourself.'

'Miss Marsh has been extremely helpful. Impressively so, in fact.' The Boss was looking at me over a transcript of Penny's debrief, which was a good half-inch thick. Her MI5 file was sitting on his desk as well, marked with the black stripe that indicated a deceased officer. It looked like Penny wasn't coming back from the dead.

'Have you decided what to do about her, sir? Can't we send her back to Five?'

'She's already dead. Putting her back now would raise too many questions.'

'Then what about resettlement? She did me right in there, sir. I was glad of the support.'

'It's already decided.'

'Oh.' The envelope was sitting next to her personnel file – I must have been ignoring it. 'What's going to happen?'

'She's already dead. It seems foolish not to take advantage of that.'

'Right.'

'Is there a problem?'

'No, sir.'

'Good. Because you're going to take care of it.' My stomach fell through the floor. I suppose the Boss wanted to make sure I hadn't lost my nerve or something, but at that moment I'd rather have shot him than Penny Marsh.

'Yes, sir.'

'Orders.' He slid the envelope across to me.

'Written orders?'

'Given the nature of the assignment, they're required.' This was a new one on me, but my orders normally came as part of a case file. I opened the envelope and read the single sheet of pale-green paper it held.

Not what I wanted to see, by a long shot. I should have left her with Martin.

Penny was being held at a safe house just outside Basingstoke, close enough for the London bods to get to her but nicely out of the way in case she caused a fuss. It wasn't much to look at outside, but like many of these places all the good stuff was underground.

'Hello, Penny.' I was trying to be cheerful – I gave myself about a seven out of ten for the impersonation.

'I was wondering where you were. Enjoying your leave?'

'Not yet. Loose ends.'

'Like me?'

'Like you.'

'So what happens now? Another bag over my head?'

'Not this time. There's a car waiting.'

I drove us out into the country, taking it slow as we enjoyed the scenery and talked over what had happened. She asked exactly what I really did, and I decided to tell her.

'You're kidding.'

'Not this time.'

'I refuse to believe we've got bloody wizards farting around with that much power. I've seen witches, and they're just a bunch of well-meaning hippies with delusions of grandeur. Where's your magic wand, then?'

'It's not like that.' Except when it is, of course, but I didn't see any point in confusing the issue.

'Guns, wands and a licence to do whatever you want, including order me around. Can't you just tell me the truth?'

'I've got no reason to lie to you, Penny. It's not like you're going to tell anyone.'

'Oh.' I think it finally hit her, then: the idea that she was about to die. 'Where are we going?'

'Somewhere out of the way. You'll see soon enough.'

'Right.'

'It could be worse, you know.'

'I suppose so. Do me a favour though, will you?'

'If I can.'

'Make it quick.'

'That's up to you.'

'Right.'

We drove on for another half-hour, not saying a word. Finally we came to the turn-off, and I pulled into the lane. Penny was scared, now, but I had to give her credit for holding herself together. Most people facing the end of their lives would be blubbing by now, begging for a few more precious seconds. Penny had more grit than that.

At the end of the drive was a house. Old, not exactly pretty or well kept. An anonymous place where anonymous things happened to anonymous people. We got out of the car and climbed the steps, then passed through the door. It wasn't the first time I'd been here, and I remembered how I felt when it had been.

In the hallway was a group of people. Middle-aged, tough, scary people. Some of them could rip your spleen out with a fingernail. Penny looked at them, then at me.

'What's this?'

The Boss stepped forward from the centre of the group, extending his hand.

'Welcome to the Service, Miss Marsh.' I turned and walked away before she had time to reply.

She caught up with me just as I started the car.

'What the fuck is going on?'

'You heard the man. Welcome to Hell.'

'And that's it? You just drive off and leave me here?'

'Yep.'

'I don't even know your name.'

'Call me Jack,' I said. 'You'll be calling me far worse before all this is over.'

THE END
of **Eagle Rising**

Jack will be back in
Turnabout